# THE FAMILY JEWELS

BRUCE F. KATZ

Cover and interior layout by Blue Pen

ISBN: 979-8-218-11787-0 (paperback)
ISBN: 979-8-218-11788-7 (ebook)

# Also from Bruce F. Katz

## Non-Fiction

*When Your Name Is on the Door*

Vito Calabrese stared at the receiver in his hand before hanging up the phone. *Kid never did that before*, he thought.

"Angelo," he said, "go to your mother's, now!" He caught his nephew's eye and gestured toward the door.

At twenty-four, Angelo Telentino was far enough along in his uncle's organization to know not to ask questions. He left Uncle Vito's candy store on 18th Avenue in the Bensonhurst section of Brooklyn immediately and quick-walked the five blocks to the apartment he once shared with his mother, his brother, and the girl from Siena.

When he got home, he found his brother Johnny sitting alongside their bedridden mother, holding her hand. She was barely more than a gray-skinned skeleton. Both sons knew what was coming.

"I'm not dead yet, Angelo," she whispered. "Any minute, but not yet."

"I know, Mom," he said. She opened her eyes. It was work for her.

Minutes earlier, before they heard her oldest son bounding up the hallway stairs, she made sure Johnny hid the box he'd removed from her bottom bureau drawer. She also had him remove two large manila envelopes from her nightstand.

"Johnny," she whispered, "give your brother . . ." It was all she could do to say even a few words.

Each of the envelopes had a name label. Johnny handed Angelo his.

"What's this?" Angelo asked.

"Johnny . . ." she said.

John Telentino wiped his eyes on the sleeve of his pale blue button-down Oxford shirt. The apartment smelled of garlic; the girl, Violetta Mazzarese, was making gravy for their dinner. She'd come to the US from the old country nearly a year earlier to help care for Maria Telentino.

"These are trust accounts Pop had Uncle Vito set up for us before he . . . died," Johnny said. "We don't have to do anything. Pete DeSantis is handling it all."

Angelo looked inside his envelope. "How much?"

Johnny shook his head. "Doesn't matter," he said. "You can access yours next year, after you turn twenty-five. I'll be able to get to mine when I finish at seminary."

"Father Johnny," Angelo said, smirking. "Can't believe you're going through with that. Where's the girl?"

The girl working in the kitchen had been inconsolable since Dr. Caputo left two hours earlier. He had told her and Johnny to keep Maria comfortable. He'd also said she'd probably pass before the sun set over Lower New York Bay.

Violetta had come to Brooklyn from Siena in Italy when Maria Telentino first learned the cancer had metastasized beyond her colon to her liver and pancreas. She was deaf but could read lips and speak, although not much in English. She loved Maria and she adored Johnny. She was terrified of Angelo.

Johnny ignored his brother's question. "Do you think, maybe, you could sit with Mom while I go to the bathroom?"

"Go," Angelo said. He looked at his mother but didn't sit down. "She's not going anywhere."

When Johnny came back to his mother's bedroom her eyes were closed. Angelo was going through the drawers of her bureau. "Where are they?" he asked.

Violetta came into Maria's room. "Is she . . . ?"

"No, Violetta," Johnny said. "Not yet."

Angelo slammed the bottom bureau drawer. "Where are they?"

"Where are what?" Violetta asked Johnny.

Johnny didn't answer. He took his mother's hand. It was cold. He put his cheek down near her nose. Nothing. He looked at his brother, then at Violetta. He shook his head. She started crying.

"I asked you a fucking question, Johnny," Angelo said.

"She's gone, Angelo," Johnny said. "And they're safe, somewhere you'll never get your filthy hands on them."

Angelo glared at his brother. "This ain't high school, Johnny. This is the real fucking world."

"Yes, it is, and in the real world I can still kick your miserable ass, Angelo."

Angelo left through the front door of the apartment and went down the hallway stairs. Violetta melted into Johnny's arms. The two of them stayed like that, weeping, for several minutes.

Maria Telentino died on Tuesday, September 7, 1982. They'd known she was going, so Johnny had taken care of her final arrangements. She'd be buried at Green-Wood Cemetery near Prospect Park on Friday the tenth. Violetta had a prepaid ticket for Sunday evening on Alitalia out of JFK to Rome. Someone from her family would pick her up and drive her the three hours home to Siena. Johnny wasn't scheduled to leave for the seminary until early the following day, so he'd personally get her to the airport and onto her flight.

When Johnny and Violetta cleaned out the apartment, they found Maria had cash squirreled away all over the place. By the time they'd gone through coffee cans, face powder containers, kitchen canisters, freezer bags, and shoe boxes, Johnny had amassed nearly $1,300 in ones, fives, tens, and a few twenties. He'd use the cash to take taxis wherever he needed to go in order to close down his and Violetta's lives in Brooklyn. Angelo had been living away from home for the past two years and probably wouldn't be using the apartment at all now that his mother was gone.

On Thursday, John was at Green-Wood finalizing details for his mother's burial the next day. Violetta stayed at the apartment packing both of their bags for their respective flights on Sunday and Monday. Johnny had booked rooms for them at the Hilton near LaGuardia. Neither of them had much in the way of belongings. Patrick Fenton Seminary discouraged acolytes from bringing much of the world into their education, and Violetta had brought very little with her when she arrived from Italy. On Saturday, movers would come to collect the furniture and household goods and place everything into storage at a family-owned warehouse in Bay Ridge.

After she finished with the bags, Violetta went into Maria's room and stared at the bed. She had come to love the woman she'd served and had hoped to return home to Italy after a much longer stay in America.

She felt a presence behind her but didn't have time to react before she was thrown down onto the empty bed.

"Nobody here, Violetta?" Angelo asked. He ripped off her floral-print dress, revealing Violetta's petite, shapely, nineteen-year-old body. She was wearing a white bra and plain cotton panties. She kicked at him and tried twisting out of his grip.

"*Per favore*, Angelo," she said, weeping.

"Mm, mm, mm," he said. "I have been imagining this day. No old lady, no Father Johnny, just you and me. Just you and me." He tore off her panties.

"No," she said, but she knew Angelo never took no for an answer. She tried to scratch at his face, but he quickly turned her over and held her down with his left arm across the back of her neck while he stepped out of his pants. He climbed onto her before she could slip from his grip. He weighed almost twice as much as she did. He took her from behind, brutally. She was a virgin. There was a lot of blood.

After he began to dress, she turned herself over and got off the bed. She stood up straight and glared at him. "*Sei una bestia. Un maiale sporco,*" she said.

He turned around and faced her. He was smiling. "Sticks and stones—"

She kicked him in the balls, hard as she could. He may have torn off her dress and panties, but he hadn't thought about her clunky black leather pumps with low heels. He grabbed at his crotch, leaving his face unprotected. She slapped and punched him six or seven times until he managed to hit her hard, with the back of his hand. This knocked her back onto the bed.

"You fucking little dago bitch," he said, and punched her, first in the face and then in her left temple.

"*Bastardo! Pezzo di merda,*" she said. "You will die for your sins!"

He stared at her. "Not before I'm finished with you," he said.

For another hour, Angelo raped and beat the young Italian girl. When he was done, he threw her, unconscious, onto the floor of the apartment's foyer.

"Let Johnny deal with you, you fucking whore," he shouted. "Now no one in the old country will have anything to do with you."

There was a mirror just inside the front door of the apartment. Angelo looked at his face, touching a scratch on his cheek and a slight bruise under his left eye.

"Little bitch," he muttered.

Johnny returned to find Violetta on the floor.

"Oh, Angelo," he said, and knelt down. He touched her cheek. She opened her eyes. At first, she recoiled, then she nodded and began to cry. Johnny held her. "I'm so sorry, sweetheart," he said. "I'm so, so sorry. Was it . . . ?"

"Angelo," she whispered. His name was the last word Violetta Mazzarese would speak out loud.

# CHAPTER 1

## October 2016

Father Mike moved without the ball, easing slowly to his left. Deshaun, the community college kid guarding him, turned his attention to the priest's teammate, another Kingsborough student. This one drove into the lane, leaving Father Mike wide open. Marquis, the big guy down in the post, took a bounce pass from the guy driving the lane. He touch-passed it to Father Mike. Deshaun tried to recover. The priest dribbled once, faked, rose up, and drained a fifteen-foot jumper. He smiled and pointed a finger.

"In basketball, you gotta stay with your man, Deshaun, not the ball. Especially a high-percentage shooter like me," the smiling priest said.

"Next time, Padre," Deshaun said. He shook his finger and mock-glared. "Next time, old man."

Father Mike clutched at his heart. "Old man? C'mon, I'm thirty-three," he said.

He walked with the boys from the schoolyard basketball court, across E. 12th Street to the side entrance
of one of Brooklyn's largest Roman Catholic churches.
"See you guys Thursday for catechism, right?" They
nodded and smiled as they fist-bumped the priest.
The five young black men headed down E. 12th Street
toward Kings Highway.

Father Mike walked through the office entrance of the
large granite building. He took no notice of a black
Cadillac CTS parked in the driveway alongside an old
house across Avenue O. The car faced the street and
the front of St. Brendan's.

"You ready for this, Bobby?"

"You gotta promise he's not gonna get hurt, Junior."

"If it goes like I planned, and if he doesn't do anything stupid, nobody gets hurt and we make a lot of
money," said Angelo Telentino Jr.

"He's a good guy, Father Mike," said Bobby Quattrone. "Makes me want to be a better Catholic. You
gotta promise, Junior."

"First, you know my name is Angelo. Only my father calls me Junior. Second, we're all good Catholics,
Bobby, at least on Sunday. Third, just do what the fuck
I say, okay? Suit up." They pulled on thin, tight-fitting
black leather gloves.

Father Mike left through the office door of St.
Brendan's dressed in his black cassock. He crossed

Avenue O and walked up E. 12th Street toward Avenue N. He carried a Domino Supermarket sack containing blue bank bags with the Easter Sunday Mass offerings. The bag also had something else inside, something way more valuable than the cash and checks. Normally, church volunteers tallied the collections and took the deposits to the bank. Since this was the Monday after Easter Sunday, and since he was carrying something for the bishop's safe deposit box, Father Mike was making the trip by himself, as he had on previous special occasions.

"Okay, here we go," Junior said. He pulled out of the driveway, turned left onto Avenue O, and then left again onto E. 13th Street. He raced to the corner and took another left onto Avenue N. He turned left once more onto E. 12th Street, a tree-lined street with single- and two-family homes. Cars were parked only on the east side of the street due to the City's street-sweeping rules. About halfway down the street, Junior slipped the CTS into a space next to a hydrant.

He and Bobby pulled rubber Bill Clinton masks over their heads and exited the car behind the priest. Junior ran in front of Father Mike while Bobby got on his hands and knees behind him.

"Give it up, old man," Junior said, attempting to sound young and black.

Father Mike stared at him. "What is up with the 'old man' stuff today?" he said, smiling.

In a quick, practiced move, Junior shoved the priest

in the chest. Father Michael missed falling over Bobby, but he tripped over the curb and fell backward, hitting his head hard, first on the hydrant, and then, with a sickening crack, on the cement sidewalk. Junior grabbed the shopping bag. Bobby stumbled to his feet. They ran. They didn't look back to take note of the blood pooling around the back of Father Mike's head. Instead, they rushed into the Caddy and sped away. The whole episode lasted less than twenty seconds.

They took their masks off. Junior pounded the steering wheel. "Can't you do one fucking thing right?"

"He's okay, right, Junior? Angelo? Right?" Bobby asked.

Junior looked at Bobby. "He's got a headache is all."

They parked on Elm Avenue. Junior opened the blue bank bag he'd removed from the brown shopping bag. "Let's see what we got."

There was a sizable wad of checks in the bag. Junior handed them to Bobby. "Tear these into small pieces," he said, "and get rid of them in the dumpster behind Domino." He opened a small manila envelope and took out another, smaller envelope filled with cash. He quickly counted $1,500 and looked at Bobby. "Looks like about seven hundred." He peeled off $200 in tens and twenties. "Here ya go," he said. "Your share, even though you didn't do your damn job."

Finally, he got to the third bag, a beige velvet drawstring pouch. He opened it and stared at the contents for a few seconds. "Okay, let's get the fuck out of here."

Junior drove for three blocks, turned onto E. 17th Street, then a quick left into the alley behind the food market. He stopped the car alongside three dumpsters in a row. He looked at Bobby. "You waiting for Christmas?" Bobby got out and slipped the empty Domino's bag into the first trash dumpster. He sprinkled the torn checks into the second dumpster. The masks and gloves went into the third. Bobby came back and got into the car.

"Okay, listen to me. This is very important," Junior said, handing Bobby the beige pouch. He jabbed his finger at Bobby. "You take this bag, you don't open it, you don't look at it, you hide it somewhere safe in your apartment. Somewhere your bitch sister won't find it and you won't forget where you put it. Until I talk to you again, I don't know you, and you don't know me. Understand?"

"I understand, Junior. I'm not stupid."

"I'm not gonna debate that with you right now, Bobby. In a few days, when we're done, there'll be a shitload more money, and you'll be able to get out from under Barbara's thumb. Now, what did I tell you to do?"

"I thought you liked her," Bobby said.

"Yeah, sometimes," Junior said. "Sometimes I want to kill her. Now, what did I tell you to do?"

Junior dropped Bobby off a couple of blocks from his apartment building on E. 14th Street and drove away. Bobby looked at the cash Junior had given him. He vaulted up the three flights of stairs and unlocked the front door. The apartment was empty. He went directly to his sister's bedroom closet and retrieved a cardboard box from a high shelf. He placed the pouch into the box under a cache of letters tied with a blue ribbon. He left his building and walked slowly back to where they'd robbed Father Mike.

Several dozen onlookers, mostly children, parents, and teachers who'd come down the street from PS 199, watched as the chaos of a crime scene unfolded on E. 12th Street. Bobby was on the Avenue N side of the crime scene tape. Another gaggle formed on the Avenue O side of the scene, where NYPD blue-and-whites from the 71st Precinct and a NY1 news truck had parked, all facing the wrong direction on the one-way street. The media could sniff out a story before it even started to smell. Reporters yelled questions at cops. The cops ignored the reporters.

A middle-aged woman, dark brown hair salted with gray, dark brown eyes filled with tears, her right hand in front of her mouth, watched from behind the curtains of an upstairs window in a house on the east side of the street. She wept silently, alone, but her vision was acute, and her memory, to her dismay, was perfect.

The EMT stood and signaled forensic technicians that they could examine the scene. He turned to the slim, light-skinned African American detective in charge and said, "Blunt-force trauma to the back of the head, Lieutenant."

Detective Lieutenant Quinn Otis said, "Mazilli, you and Koch grab a couple of uniforms and canvas these houses. See if anyone saw anything. We need to know if this priest just tripped and fell or if something else happened."

Walking as quickly as his eighty-year-old legs would take him, a priest pushed his way to the barricade and asked Detective Lieutenant Otis if he could see Father Mike.

"I don't know, Father . . ."

"Wakely. James Wakely. I'm a pastor at St. Brendan's. Father Michael is my associate."

"It's not good, Father," Otis said, lifting the yellow tape. He walked Father James around the EMT wagon to where the forensics team was working the scene. Father James knelt and whispered words over the young priest's body. It wasn't last rites; those were reserved for the dying, not the already dead.

"Have you got the bag he was carrying?" Father James asked.

Otis yelled to the patrol officers who were first on the scene and asked about a bag. They both shook their heads. Father James let out a deep sigh. "Father Michael was going to the bank on Avenue M." He stared at the covered body on the ground. "He'd just finished playing basketball with several young parishioners. It's something he loved doing."

"It's all right, Father," Otis said. "Anything you can tell me now will help us figure out what happened here and hopefully get back whatever is missing."

Father James closed his eyes, bowed his head, took in a deep breath, and let it out. How could he explain what happened? Not only to the police but also to the bishop. He revealed the delicate nature of the situation to the detective.

"Do you have a picture?" Otis asked.

"I'll get one to you. What happens now?" the old priest said.

"There'll be an autopsy," Otis said. "Later today, maybe. Then the body will be released. I'll do my best to make it happen as quickly as possible. Does he have any relatives?"

Father James thought for a moment. "I'll . . . we'll . . . you know, I'm not sure. He definitely has no relatives living here. Let me check on that. For the most part, we're the family Father Michael had."

Otis offered his condolences. Father James walked back to St. Brendan's and called the bishop.

Bobby watched it play out. His was just another face in a crowd of onlookers. It wasn't the only face stained with tears; Father Mike was beloved in the neighborhood, even by those who weren't members at St. Brendan's or who weren't even Catholic. Inconsolable, Bobby stepped away from the scene and walked back to his apartment.

St. Brendan's was a focal point in the neighborhood. A requiem Mass would take place here right after the police released Father Michael's remains. Father James prayed in one of the pews and John Telentino, bishop of the Diocese of Brooklyn, knelt alongside him.

When they finished praying, the bishop said, "Lieutenant Otis told me they have no idea what happened. I told him we'd cooperate in any way we could."

Father James had to tread lightly, but the question needed to be asked. "Will you be calling . . . your brother?"

The bishop gave him a quick sidelong look, then his expression softened. "I suppose I'll have to, Jimmy, for a couple of reasons."

# CHAPTER 2

Joshua Abrahams sat at his desk in the open newsroom at the *St. Louis Post* finishing a story involving a home invasion and double murder in the ordinarily quiet suburb of Creve-Coeur. His computer pinged a notification from the newspaper's national desk. It contained a photo link and a series of question marks. He clicked the photo open and leaned in to closely examine a headshot of one Father Michael Olivetti, thirty-three. The priest had been found dead on a Brooklyn street earlier that day. He stared at the face for a moment before he grabbed his mobile. He punched a number on speed dial.

"Hey, I thought you were on deadline," his father said.

"I'm always on deadline, every day, Dad. Can you meet me at Doyle's?"

"Sure. You okay?" his father asked.

"Yeah, I think so. Dad?"

"Yeah?" There was a long silence on the line. "Josh?"

"Yeah, I'm here."

Joshua paused. He stared again at the image of the murdered young priest. "Dad, I think we may have found him."

Thirty-three years earlier, a rape victim housed at Patrick Fenton Seminary had given birth to healthy twin boys. Patrick Fenton—located just outside of St. Louis in Shrewsbury, Missouri—was one of the places in the United States where young men came to complete the educational process necessary to be ordained as priests in the Roman Catholic Church.

Back then, along with another dozen or so other young acolytes, John Telentino arrived from Brooklyn. Just twenty-two, he was angry and psychologically shaken. He brought with him to the seminary a few personal items and a BA in theology from St. John's University. He also arrived with a young Italian girl who had been brutally attacked just days earlier. The assault had been so violent it rendered Violetta Mazzarese, already deaf from a birth defect, unable to speak. The young woman found sanctuary at the seminary. A few weeks after her arrival she learned she was pregnant. A few weeks after that, she learned she was carrying twin boys.

Henry and Michelle Abrahams were moderately observant Jews living near Forest Park in St. Louis. Shelley taught high school English; Henry had a solo law practice. He specialized in wills, trusts, and family law. Childless in their late thirties, they leaped at the chance to adopt one of the boys. They named their son, their only child, Joshua.

When Joshua was five, the archbishop of the St. Louis diocese welcomed the Abrahams' application to send him to Catholic school. They also made sure Joshua learned what it meant to be Jewish. As a result, lasagna and matzo ball soup were served at Josh's bar mitzvah.

The other baby boy, named Michael by the sisters at the seminary, found a home with the Olivetti's, an older, also childless family related to a monsignor from a diocese across the Mississippi River, near Alton, Illinois. Michael grew up attending Catholic school and obtained a BA in theology from St. Louis University.

Doyle's was buzzing at 5:15 p.m. The St. Louis hangout, located near the corner of Pine and N. Sixth Street in the downtown heart of the city, attracted media types plus a mishmash of professional sports figures, politicians, and other community players. The menu included food, drink, and a stream of off-the-record conversation.

Josh and his father pulled from their bottles of Budweiser; in St. Louis it was a venial sin to drink anything else. Josh produced the picture and accompanying news story involving the death of Father Michael Olivetti.

Henry took in a deep breath. "Good looking kid," he said, shaking his head. "Reminds me of someone I knew before he went all ZZ Top. Too bad, what happened."

Josh nodded and stroked his nicely manicured short dark brown facial hair. "I checked out a picture of me before I grew my beard." He smiled. "One face."

"What do you know?" his father asked.

"What you've got there is all I know," Josh said, "for now." Henry raised his eyebrows.

"For now?"

"Yeah. I'm heading to Brooklyn tomorrow. There's a legit St. Louis connection. At the very least, he went to Patrick Fenton. Jasper gave me a week to make something out of it."

"Why you?" Henry asked.

"Well, for one, I'm a reporter covering crime, cops, and courts. And . , ," Josh hesitated. "I showed Jasper the picture, and he couldn't speak for about thirty seconds."

"When do you leave?"

"I'm booked on United at noon. I have an early session with Christopher, then I'll be on my way."

"Is there any higher you can go in that . . . what's it called?"

"RMA, Dad. Reality martial arts," Josh said. "And no, there isn't any higher I can go. Now I do it for fun and for exercise. But you know, since I'm heading for Brooklyn, my first time in big bad New York City, I should probably know how to deal with all kinds of potential threats to my well-being, right?"

"Yeah, yeah, big shot," Henry said.

"No, no," Josh said. "You know, what Christopher teaches is not classroom karate, Dad. We learn how to handle real situations, not bowing and pulling punches."

"Okay, killer," Henry said, surrendering. "Go. Learn." He picked up the picture of the slain priest. "Just be careful, okay? Stuff happens."

"Always, Dad."

At six weeks, when the Abrahams' got their first look at the twins, it came down to a coin-flip kind of decision which one to adopt. What the Abrahams didn't know after choosing Josh, and hadn't learned since, was the disposition of the other twin or anything at all about the birth parents.

"Your mother looped in?"

"Not yet," Josh said. They finished their Buds, got into their cars, jumped onto I-64, and headed west toward Chesterfield, where Henry and Shelley lived.

Bobby Quattrone was trying to hold things together, but was failing, miserably. Living with his older sister was tough on a good day. He did everything he could to avoid her, either by staying out of their small four-room apartment as much as possible or cloistering himself in his small bedroom.

He couldn't avoid the facts, though. He was at least partially responsible for Father Michael's death, and the bag from the robbery was in his sister's closet. At least he was sure she wouldn't find it. He'd put it at the bottom of a box of stuff that belonged to their mother. And he knew Barbara wouldn't disturb those memories under any circumstances.

"Bobby! You gotta come out and eat. I got work to do. I need to get into the city, and I can't wait for you."

"You go ahead," he said through his door. "I'll take care of myself."

"I know you're upset about Father Mike, Bobby." Now she sounded like she was just outside the door. "We all are. Just do your best to move on. He didn't believe in self-pity, you know." She wouldn't open the door to his room. It was part of their deal to respect each other's boundaries.

Bobby couldn't stop the tears. He prayed she'd leave if he just stayed silent. "I'll be home around nine tonight," she said. "You take care. I love you." He heard her close and lock the front door. The only thing Bobby knew for sure was that he needed to stay away from Junior.

Angelo Jr. felt like a stranger in a strange land. He found himself on Atlantic Avenue, several subway stops from his Flatbush neighborhood and, culturally, in an entirely different world. Leaving a Duane

Reade pharmacy where he bought a cheap untraceable cell phone for cash, he approached a black kid, maybe twelve years old, and offered him twenty dollars to make a call. He had already written down the phone number and the words he wanted the kid to say.

"Ask for Father James," he said. The kid took the twenty and dialed the number.

"Uh, listen here, if you want your stuff back, get a quar—uh, quarter-million dollars and wait for another call. You feel me? You got two days." The kid returned the phone to Junior. He put it to his ear.

"Who is this? Who is this?" the old priest said. "Did you kill Father Michael, you . . . you—"

Angelo disconnected the call and walked away. Before throwing the burner into a sewer, he placed a call to the 71st Precinct.

"Seven-one, Devlin," the desk officer answered.

"Yeah, listen, I saw a few black kids running down E. 12th Street just around the time that priest got killed. They looked like the same kids who played basketball with the priest, you know?" He hung up.

Father James stared at his phone for a few seconds before dialing the number of the bishop's private cell. By the time his call went to voice mail, Bishop Telentino appeared in the doorway of the sacristy at St. Brendan's.

"John, I was just calling you. There's a . . . situation," the old priest said.

"You mean robbery and Michael's murder aren't enough?"

"I'm sorry. I just received a phone call. It sounded like a ransom demand."

"Tell me exactly what was said. Exactly, Jimmy."

Father James recounted the call perfectly, even the "you feel me" part. "Should we contact Detective Otis?" he asked.

John sighed. "Someone thinks he knows what he's stolen, Jimmy," he said. "I need to contact my brother. We'll call the police later."

Nothing turned up on the police canvass of homes on E. 12th Street. No one was home, no one answered, or those who did answer had nothing to say.

Intense media coverage surrounded the young priest's death. The theft of the bank bags made the crime a homicide during the commission of a robbery. At the bishop's request, the police held back mention of what exactly was stolen. They concentrated on the cash in the bank bag. The powers at One Police Plaza leaned hard on the precinct commander. He, in turn, leaned hard on Detective Lieutenant Otis.

Officers followed up on the anonymous tip about the black kids running from the scene. The secretary at St. Brendan's knew who they were and quickly dismissed any possibility that they could have been involved with what happened to Father Mike.

"You're wasting your time, detectives," she told them. "Father Mike worked personally with Deshaun, Marquis, and the others for over a year."

Detectives ultimately came to the same conclusion. They caught up with the five of them at the Kingsborough campus in Manhattan Beach. All five were good kids, good students, and totally devastated by what had happened to Father Mike.

"What that means," Otis told his squad, "is that someone purposely tried to throw us off course. We need to scrub that call."

Newspaper reporters and television news crews crawled all over the quiet residential neighborhood. They did their own canvass near the scene. Every day, on every early and late newscast, some fair-haired, blue-eyed reporter would be live, reporting breathlessly from St. Brendan's or on E. 12th Street, where Father Michael had been robbed and killed, or in front of one of the homes where someone had absolutely nothing to add to the mystery. This kind of story—the robbery and murder of a young, beloved priest—wouldn't go away until something bigger and messier happened.

# CHAPTER 3

"Well, isn't this special?" Angelo Telentino Sr. said. "The big important bishop finally learned how to use a telephone." He paused. "How long has it been, Johnny? How many years?" Another pause. "Listen, I'm sorry about the kid, the priest." Bishop John Telentino looked to the heavens, managing to hold his tongue.

"Can you find out who did this?" he asked.

His brother let out a sigh. "You think I know everything that happens in Brooklyn?" he asked. "I'll check around. They got the jewels, right?"

"We got a ransom call. They want a quarter-million dollars."

"I told you back then, you should have given them to me. Tell you what, Johnny, let me handle this."

"Handle what?"

"The money . . . the whole thing. I'll find out who did this, but first I'll get the money from DeSantis."

"No, no, no, Angelo, I'll handle that. Remember, I have money of my own. You don't need to get involved in the money. Please, just see if you can learn who did this." They both hung up.

Ignoring his younger brother, as he had since they were kids, Angelo dialed a number in Fort Lauderdale, Florida.

## November 1978

The Telentino brothers, Angelo and John, were always distinct entities. They shared parents but little else. Angelo was four years older, but he never embraced the role of benevolent big brother. In fact, until he started working for their uncle, Vito Calabrese, Angelo either ignored or tormented young Johnny.

They both attended parochial school in Bay Ridge. Until junior high, when John caught up physically, Angelo was always bigger, stronger, and meaner than his quiet, sensitive kid brother. John was never mean, but he did grow, and he did get stronger.

"He's like his father," Maria often told John. "You're more like me."

"Why does he have to be so mean to me? We're both your sons, right?"

When Angelo was a senior at St. Patrick's, on 97th Street and 4th Avenue, and Johnny was a freshman, Angelo showed up at a tryout for the school's wrestling team. John had his eye on joining the school team as a middleweight.

"Really, Johnny?" Angelo said. "You? A wrestler?"

John hoped he'd get bored and leave.

"Come here," Angelo said, removing his jacket. "Show me what you got."

The coach smiled. Brother Daniel was a big freckle-faced, red-haired Irish novice. He gestured for John to mix it up with his older brother. "Show him what you've got, Johnny."

John walked over to the bench where his brother was flexing and putting on a show for some of his friends. "You really want to do this, Angelo?"

"Do you?" Angelo said.

"I don't want to make you look bad in front of your crew here," John said.

"Look at you!" his brother said, laughing. "Come on, kid, gimme your best."

John removed his shoes and walked to the center of the mat. He stood there, waiting for his brother. He kept his face neutral. No fear, no bravado. Angelo finished showing off for his pals. He took his black leather loafers off, walked onto the wrestling mat, and assumed a boxing stance.

"You know what wrestling is, right Angelo?" John asked, circling his brother while shaking his hands and arms loose. The brothers were nearly the same size and weight. Angelo had been a scrapper since grade school. John was always more collegial than confrontational.

"Yeah," he said. "Wrestling is guys in their underwear grabbing each other by the crotch. You want to fight, let's fight, Johnny."

John came in low, grabbed his brother around the waist and threw him to the mat. It was a quick move that caught Angelo by surprise and drew a smile from Brother Daniel. A crowd formed around the mat.

Angelo got to his feet. He was pissed off. "You suckered me, kid," he said, pointing a finger. "Now I'm really gonna teach you a lesson."

John smiled at his brother. "You can stop whenever you want, big brother," he said. "No one will think any less of you."

Angelo stepped in and tried to grab his brother around the head and neck. John ducked away, caught Angelo around the waist from behind, and threw him to the canvas mat again with a quick grab-and-trip move.

"Okay," Brother Daniel said. "We need to stop this. One of you knows what he's doing and one of you doesn't. I don't want to see anyone get hurt here."

"Stay back, Brother Daniel," Angelo said. He got to his feet and glared at John.

Angelo came at John again, but once again he stayed high. This time, though, he turned John around and managed to land a hard punch to his brother's shoulder.

"This is wrestling, Angelo," Brother Daniel said, "not street fighting."

John smiled at Angelo. "Come on, big brother," he

said. "Is that the best you've got?" John egged him on, gesturing for his brother to mix it up.

"Come on, Angelo," one of his friends said. "He's your kid brother."

"Mind your fucking business, Joey," Angelo said.

"That's enough," Brother Daniel said, stepping onto the mat between the two brothers.

John stepped off the mat and walked over to the seats alongside the gymnasium floor. He picked up his jacket.

"What's the matter, punk?" Angelo said to him. "You afraid of me?"

"Yeah, Angelo," John said over his shoulder. "Afraid of making you look bad in front of your friends." He turned around. "Next time, I won't go so easy on you."

The brothers looked at each other. Angelo laughed and nodded. "All right, Johnny," he said. "All right."

"Tomorrow okay, Brother Daniel?" John asked.

"No need, John," he said. "You're on the team."

The Telentino brothers never physically confronted one another again.

## October 2016

Billy DeSantis couldn't answer his cell phone. He was too busy getting the shit kicked out of him. "Fuck, Milos," he said. "If you kill me, you'll never get your money."

"I'm not going to kill you, Billy. But I'm going to make sure you understand the seriousness of this situation we got," Milos Alvarez said, removing the thin leather gloves from his hands. "You got some issues, Billy. You're a bad gambler, man. You need to pay your fucking debts. You got three days, and then I start breakin' stuff."

"It's cash flow, Milos, not a gambling problem," Billy said.

"Not knowing when to stop hanging out with the Panamanians in Dania, the ponies at Gulfstream, and the dogs in Kendall isn't cash flow, Billy. It's a sickness. You don't have to—ah, what's the use. Like I said, you need to pay your fucking bill."

Later, when Billy checked his messages, he groaned when he saw one from Angelo Telentino. "What does this jerk-off want?" he said aloud.

*"Billy D., Angelo Telentino. Listen, I need you to bring me two fifty K as soon as possible. Let me know when you'll be here. We'll have dinner, maybe a little fun. Remember, two fifty K in cash, ASAP."*

He was listening to the message a second time when another call rang in.

"Fuck! Him too?" Billy DeSantis managed money for both Telentino brothers. They had legacy accounts, compliments of Vito Calabrese, their late uncle on their mother's side. Vito had been a made man, a capo, dead since the late eighties.

"This is Bill DeSantis."

"Hello, Billy, it's John Telentino."

"Hi, Bishop. How are things in the Big Apple?"

"We've had better times, Billy," John said. "I need you to bring a quarter-million dollars in cash up to me as soon as you can. Is that going to be a problem?"

*They both want $250,000 in cash?*

"No, not at all, sir," Billy said. "I'll get back to you when I have specifics. It should be in the next day or two."

This wasn't a problem. But he considered the possibility it might be an opportunity. He made an Amtrak reservation, and then he called Milos.

Billy didn't keep up on the news of the day, and Billy didn't fly.

Barbara Quattrone was driving east on Avenue O when she spotted Bobby coming out of St. Brendan's. Tears were streaming down his face. She couldn't stop in time, so she circled the block as quickly as possible. When she returned to the front of the church and parked, her brother was gone. She went inside and cornered Father James.

"Father, I just saw my brother leave the church crying. What happened?"

"I don't know, Barbara. I just got back myself. He must have come in while I was out giving communion over at the nursing home on Coney Island Avenue."

"He's my brother, Father," she said. "I'm all he's got,

and he's all I've got. He's been a mess since, ah, you know. I really need him to be all right."

"You need to talk to him, Barbara. He's an adult. If there's something he wants you to know, I'm sure he'll tell you."

"You gotta tell me what's going on, Bobby," Barbara said. "You lock yourself in your room. Then I see you leaving St. Brendan's looking like someone who was about to get what Jesus got. Now I catch you coming out of my room, which you know you should never go into in the first place. What's going on with you?"

Bobby sat on the sofa, looking at his feet and shaking his head.

"So," she said, hands on her hips, "let's start with why you were in my room."

Barbara and Bobby Quattrone had been living by themselves in the two-bedroom apartment on East 14th Street in Brooklyn for nearly ten years. Both their parents were gone. Eight years younger than his sister, Bobby usually slept on the living room sofa instead of in his bedroom. Barbara only had one rule, respect her privacy. That meant stay out of her room.

Bobby wasn't stupid. He was a handful of credits from a business degree at Brooklyn College, but his ambitions and interests focused mostly on the Church. Over the years he'd taken every catechism class he could. Besides altar service at Saturday and Sunday Mass, he occasionally served as a lector and trained as a Eucharistic minister. He did odd jobs for Father James and Father Mike, and he attended Mass almost every weekday morning. Mostly, he did his best to stay out of Barbara's way.

"I can't say anything," Bobby said. "If I do, he'll kill us both."

"Who'll kill us?" she asked. "What are you—Bobby, does this have anything to do with Father Mike? Bobby, what did you do? Tell me."

"It was Junior," he blurted. "It was his idea. He pushed him . . ."

"Stop! Stop! Don't say anything. Don't say another word, not now. Fuck! What were you doing in my room?"

He went back into her room, took the box of memories down from the shelf, and showed her what was inside.

"What am I gonna do, Barbara?" Bobby asked through intermittent sobs.

"These are Bishop Telentino's family's jewels," she said. "What are you—?"

"He told me not to look at them," Bobby said. "I think he wants to sell them or something. Nothing was supposed to happen, Barbara. He promised. He promised."

"Oh, man, what a fucking mess, Bobby," she said.

She walked in small circles in their living room. "We can't turn him in without turning you in. What a goddam fucking mess."

"Can't we tell his father? Maybe we should tell Mr. T."

She looked at him like he'd just stepped from a space ship. "Are you out of your mind?" she asked him. "This is his only son we're talking about. His only kid! No, Bobby, no, we can't tell his father. Jesus Christ!"

Bobby stayed quiet.

"Okay," she said. "Tell me the rest. Tell me everything. Don't leave anything out. Tell me the whole fucking story."

Joshua Abrahams arrived at LaGuardia. He grabbed a BLT, fries, and a Coke to go at the airport and ate inside a cab on the way to the Hampton Inn in Sheepshead Bay. It was still early enough after dropping his bags in his room to grab another cab to St. Brendan's. He'd get a rental car later if he needed one. One of the few things he knew about New York City was that a car wasn't necessary to get around.

The church secretary asked Father James if he'd take a few minutes to talk to a reporter from the area where Father Mike had gone to seminary.

"I don't know what to tell you," Father James said. "I'm sorry, Mr. . . ."

"Abrahams. Joshua Abrahams. I grew up in Chesterfield, outside St. Louis, not too far from Shrewsbury. What exactly was taken in the robbery, Father?"

Father James told him about the money and the checks but omitted any mention of the jewels. "The medical examiner said it was blunt-force trauma that killed him when his head hit the hydrant and the concrete curb," he said.

"When is the funeral, Father?"

"They'll release his body later this afternoon. We'll hold a service tomorrow at 11:00 a.m. Burial is private, over near Prospect Park, just Michael's church family, me, the bishop, some of the teachers, staff, and students from our school. Michael's adoptive parents divorced when he was a junior at De Smet High School in St. Louis. His mother died while he was at Patrick Fenton. Nobody knew anything about where his father was, or even if he was still alive. Father Michael didn't have any other family that we know about."

Josh nodded. "I'm not Catholic, Father, but if it's okay, I'd like to attend the service tomorrow," he said.

"Oh, of course, everyone is welcome. I'm sorry I don't have more for you. You came such a long way."

"Besides the bishop and the police, is there anyone else I should speak to?"

The old priest shook his head. "You can talk to the

vermin who did this," he said, genuflecting, "once the police catch him."

Angelo Jr. was parked across the street from the apartment building on E. 14th. Street where Bobby and Barbara lived. He grabbed his phone and punched in a number.

"Hey, Angelo. What's shaking?" Dominic Ciccone asked.

"I need you to do something for me."

"Whatever you want."

"I need you to keep an eye on someone, no, two people. For the next two, three days, maybe."

"You got it, boss," Dominic said. "Where and when?"

Barbara Quattrone's phone rang. It was Angelo Telentino Sr.

"I need something from you, Barbara," he said.

"Wow, there's a surprise, Mr. T. When might you stop needing something from me?" she asked.

He laughed. "If you're lucky, never," he said. "I pay you well for *all* your services, right, Barbara?"

Barbara made most of her money from the Telentino family businesses. She delivered stuff, mostly small packages—cash, she told herself—throughout the city for Mr. T and a few of his close associates.

On occasion, Angelo required her to provide other, more personal, services. It was those that she wished would stop.

"I have an important friend coming into town, probably tomorrow," Angelo said. "He's gonna stay at the Sherry-Netherland. I've already arranged dinner for him, and I'd like him to enjoy the rest of his night, if you understand what I mean." She understood. "But I don't want him to know I had anything to do with it. You *capisce?*"

This was the same approach he had used several years earlier when he paid her to introduce his inexperienced son to the wonders of womanhood. "Yeah, I understand, Mr. T. How big a scumbag is he?" There was no response. There was a lot of history between the Telentino and Quattrone families; some of it was not pleasant. "What I mean is, am I going to be safe with him?"

"You need to check yourself, Barbara. Remember who you're talking to."

"I'm sorry, sir," she said. "I'm just—"

"Come to my office. I have a package for you." He hung up.

# CHAPTER 4

St. Brendan's was filled to overflowing. The closed casket in front of the altar was covered with flowers. Alongside it was a poster-sized picture of the young priest. Josh stood off to the side of the nave and watched as people filed in.

Bishop Telentino and Father James presided over a beautiful service for the brother Joshua had never known. He walked outside to introduce himself to the bishop.

"Your Excellency, this is the young man from St. Louis I told you about," Father James said. "The reporter . . ."

"I'm so sorry for your loss, Bishop," Joshua said. "I didn't know Father Mike personally, but . . . I know he attended seminary at Patrick Fenton, near St. Louis. I'm writing something for the *Post* about his life."

The bishop looked deeply into Joshua's eyes. He smiled and put a hand on his arm. "Please, come by my office when you have time, Mr. Abrahams. Now is not good, obviously, but perhaps later this afternoon?" He handed Joshua a card with his address and the phone number at the diocesan office.

"I'd be honored, sir, thank you very much. I'll call before I come by."

As he turned to leave, Joshua almost knocked Barbara Quattrone down the steps in front of the church. When he reached out to grab her arm, he noticed Bobby Quattrone staring at him.

"Who are *you*?" Bobby asked, staring through his tears.

Joshua introduced himself. "I'm so sorry. I didn't see you standing there," he said to Barbara.

"Why does a reporter from St. Louis care about Father Mike's funeral?" Barbara asked.

"Father Mike grew up and went to school outside St. Louis," he said. We think our readers will be interested in both his life and his unfortunate death."

"But . . ." Bobby repeated, "Who *are* you?"

"Shut up, Bobby," his sister said. She looked back and forth from Josh to Bobby. "Didn't you hear him? He's a reporter. I'm sorry Mr. . . . ."

"It's Joshua Abrahams, but please, call me Josh," he said. "How well did you two know Father Mike?"

She caught a glimpse of Junior staring at her from the foot of the church steps.

"I don't have time for this now," she said. "You just

be careful, Mr.—Josh. Come on, Bobby." As they left, Josh took note of a young man who was now glaring at him.

Down East. 12th Street from St. Brendan's, about midway between Avenues O and N, Josh walked up and back, and up and back again along the street. Something out of the corner of his eye made him turn and look up. He caught a glimpse of slight movement before whoever was behind the curtain pulled back out of sight. Josh crossed the street, walked up three steps, and used the knocker and doorbell. No one answered. He noted the address, and then walked to Coney Island Avenue and Avenue O to flag down a taxi to the Hampton Inn to transcribe notes and prepare for his meeting with the bishop.

Barbara sat in a familiar burgundy vinyl-covered chair in front of what, to her, resembled a schoolteacher's desk. She was in her work clothes: tight jeans, running shoes and socks, and a white low-cut, scoop-necked blouse that revealed the tops of full breasts.

"Like I said on the phone, Barbara, this is a favor," said Angelo Sr. "This is something special."

They were in Angelo's office. It was three converted apartments in a sprawling building on 65th Street about three blocks east of McDonald Avenue. On the desk there was a phone with two lines and a Keurig coffee machine. Along one wall sat an old sofa and, next to the sofa, a beat-up gray recliner. On the wall near the door, a fifty-five-inch flat-screen TV had NY1 on with the sound turned down. They were alone in the office. Angelo's nephew Carmine sat on a folding chair outside the door reading *Sports Illustrated*.

Angelo's use of the word "special" gave her heartburn. To the boss, "special" usually meant putting out for someone she didn't know but who was important to him.

Barbara's relationship with Angelo Telentino Sr. was, in every sense of the word, complicated. Until she was twenty-two, the Telentino and Quattrone families had been close. As close, that is, as families involved in organized crime could be. Barbara's father, Tommy, had worked for Angelo. He'd handled most of Angelo's bookmaking operations in Brooklyn and Queens. He'd been a trusted lieutenant. Barbara's mother and Angelo's wife were distant relatives. This meant Tommy had had as much job security as was possible in a dangerous, often brutal work environment.

He'd made good money, which her mother, Vicki, spent with abandon. Especially when she ran around with Sofia, Angelo's wife, who had more money at her disposal and had always encouraged her cousin and best friend to buy, and then buy more.

On the other hand, because Tommy was literally a member of the family, there'd been resentments throughout the rest of the Telentino enterprise. Some of the more ambitious goombahs had viewed Tommy Quattrone as somehow undeserving of his status. Because he was protected, and as long as Angelo was satisfied with his work, Tommy had been okay. The two families had socialized together, and the wives had taken regular trips to Atlantic City for spa days and playing the slots.

Three cataclysmic events changed everything for Barbara and Bobby. The first, when she was sixteen, was not entirely unexpected. Her mother had warned her over the years that her father was in a dangerous business. There were some bad people who, even on good days, hadn't liked her father very much. So, when she came home from school to find her mother crying at the kitchen table, Barbara had known something bad had happened to Tommy.

"Angelo called," her mother said. "Your father was shot and killed in Far Rockaway today."

They hadn't been as close as some fathers and daughters, but Barbara loved Tommy Q., as he'd been known, and took the news harder than she'd expected. "Do they know who did this?" she asked.

Her mother smiled through the sobs. "Does it matter?" She stood up and hugged Barbara. "I'm going upstairs," she said. "Tell your brother when he gets home."

Vicki and her children had received a substantial amount of cash in the days and weeks following her father's murder. Angelo had moved them into an apartment in a very nice neighborhood and even had given them a chunk of the proceeds of the sale of the house they'd lived in, which he, Angelo, owned. This had made moving forward a little easier than might otherwise have been the case.

Of course, there hadn't been any income following Tommy's death, and Vicki had never worked a day in her life outside the home. This had been the norm inside the family. Vicki had known the money they'd been provided would ultimately run out, so she took a job working in a real estate office while Barbara began waiting tables at a restaurant connected to the Telentino family. They got by.

Because neither Barbara nor Bobby understood the inner workings of a sophisticated criminal enterprise, they hadn't been able to comprehend how anyone other than some rival, or maybe the police, would murder their father. Angelo had told Barbara's mother that some lower-level member of the family did this terrible thing, and he had dealt with it personally. Sofia Telentino later confirmed this version of the story to Vicki, who, in order to put the matter behind them once and for all, had repeated it to Barbara and Bobby. Years later, Barbara had come to understand how things really worked in the Telentino-Calabrese family, and that her father could only have been taken out with the knowledge and approval of people at or near the top.

Barbara had never experienced anything like the aftermath of the horrible traffic accident that took the lives of Vicki Quattrone and Sofia Telentino.

They'd been heading back to Brooklyn from a girls-only day in Atlantic City. They'd actually won a few dollars at the slots and blackjack tables in one of Donald Trump's dying casino operations and both had been a little tipsy. Sofia lost control of her Cadillac DTS on Highway 9, just south of Perth Amboy. The car had skated off the road and flipped over twice before landing wheels up in a drainage ditch. Neither woman had been wearing a seatbelt. Both were pronounced dead at the scene.

At the time, Barbara had been twenty-two. Bobby had been fourteen. For over a month, the two Quattrone children stayed in Angelo Telentino's house in Bay Ridge with him and his son, Angelo Jr. The four of them were showered with a seemingly never-ending outpouring of food, cash, companionship, and the kind of love reserved for members of a large, if not blood-related, Italian family.

At the time, Angelo's brother, Father John Telentino, had been parish priest at St. Brendan's in Brooklyn. He'd presided over both funerals and made himself available for all three children. He'd taken special care of Barbara and Bobby Quattrone, who he felt were both burdened first by the murder of their father and then the unfortunate accidental death of their mother. If there had been any remotely positive aspect to their parents' deaths, it was the relationship that blossomed between John Telentino and the two Quattrone children.

Angelo Sr. moved Barbara and Bobby into the apartment on East 14th Street, where they still lived. He'd told her he would take care of the rent on the apartment as long as she lived there with her brother. He'd created a job for her moving packages for him between his base of operations and people at destinations throughout the city.

Barbara came to accept the reality that her cargo might, on occasion, contain something other than flatware and small appliances. But Angelo had purchased a new, very nice Chrysler minivan, encouraged her to get other clients, and paid her sufficiently, in cash, to more than meet her and Bobby's needs. Her life circumstances had emotionally immunized her against the knowledge of her being a cog in the wheel of the Telentino family business.

## October 2003

When Barbara was twenty-three and Angelo Jr. was nineteen, Mr. T presented her with a nearly impossible, rock-versus-hard-place moral dilemma.

From the time she was very young, Barbara had been a beautiful girl with strong Italian features: long black hair; big, flashing dark brown eyes; flawless olive skin; and a head-turning body. Her looks made it difficult for her to fend off all the advances that came her way from the foot soldiers in Angelo's organization. She'd discovered sex soon after her mother's death and found she enjoyed it and had become good at it almost immediately. She made it a practice to date more than one person at a time so as to avoid becoming someone's girlfriend or, worse, someone's wife. She was sure she had some kind of reputation among the men in Angelo's organization, but she was smart, and she quickly figured out how to navigate those barracuda-infested waters.

Whenever Angelo called her into his office, it was like being called into the principal's office at school. On this occasion, he told her he thought it was time that his son had his first experience with a real woman.

"You're asking me to sleep with Junior?" Barbara asked. "Are you kidding me?"

"First, Barbara, I don't give a shit if you sleep with him. I just want you to pop his cherry," Angelo said. "Second, do I look like I'm kidding? Am I a man who kids? Third, I'm not asking."

Barbara was a quick study. She understood the price for having accepted all of Mr. T's help after her mother died. She was almost completely dependent on him for her and Bobby's living arrangements and income.

She had very little choice but to consider what he was demanding of her.

He walked around to the front of his desk and looked down at her. He wasn't very big, or tall, but she was sitting down, and, as she would come to learn, this was an intimidation tactic Mr. T commonly employed.

"Let me say it again, Barbara. I'm not asking."

"Angelo and I have been friends for a long time, Mr. T," she said. "I don't look at him that way, and I don't think he sees me that way either."

This time, he didn't smile. He just broke out laughing. "Barbara, Barbara," he said. "He's been jerking off to pictures he's painted of you in his head since he was old enough to get a hard-on. He doesn't just *see* you that way, he sees *only* you and *only* in that way. You gotta trust me on this."

This softened her resolve, knowing that she could likely control the situation, and she could maybe have a card to play with Mr. T down the road.

"I . . . I just don't want you to think of me like I'm, you know . . ." She couldn't even say the words. She went to church every Sunday and still had her first communion and confirmation dresses packed away in her apartment.

Then, and this was the kind of stuff he did that made him the unquestioned boss of the entire family, he closed the deal with her. "Barbara," he said, "listen to me. I have a dozen girls working in my organization that are older, wiser, and way more experienced than you are. I could call any of them, give them a couple of bucks, and they'd fuck his brains out and leave him for dead on his bed. That's not what I want for him. Or for you."

He picked up a tan manila envelope from his desk and placed it in her lap. "Open it," he said.

"Mr. T, please."

"Open it, Barbara. Don't make me tell you again."

She pinched the silver clip and opened the envelope. A stack of fifty-dollar bills tumbled out.

"Consider this a bonus for all the good, hard work you've done for me, Barbara," he said. "I'd never pay you to have sex with anyone, including my son. But loyalty goes a long way with me. It goes a very long way. Don't ever, ever forget that."

She never did. She did as he asked. It wasn't awful; it was kind of sweet, in fact. For a time, Angelo followed her around like a puppy hoping for one more treat. But for Barbara, this was a one-time thing. When word got out, it pretty much took her out of circulation with other members of the family. For her, that was a very good thing.

In the ensuing years, Mr. T again asked her to help him in this manner. It was infrequent, maybe a half-dozen times. It was always what he called a special circumstance. It also, over time, became painful and debasing. Even the money, and there was plenty of it, didn't help.

Angelo Sr. never hit her. He never hurt her in any

way, other than these special requests. He never took advantage of her for his own gratification. He never threatened her. But he also never came clean about what really happened to her father. He never explained why it happened, and that never sat quite right with her.

# October 2016

The leader of the Telentino-Calabrese family was lean, had a dark complexion, still had all his hair—black streaked with gray—and was always well dressed. Women found him attractive. "Every time I see you, Barbara, I wonder why you're not with my son or with some other guy who can, you know, take care of you," he said. "You're so good looking and so smart and so . . ."

"The word you're looking for is independent, Mr. T," she said. "You and my father were in business until, well, we know how that ended, right? You're not my father, and I don't want anything to do with your son or any of the assholes he associates with. You've been good to me and to my brother. For that, I do things for you. That's it."

He came out from behind his desk and sat next to her, close. His knee touched hers and as always, he could see down the front of her blouse. "You know, I take a lot of shit from you because of your father," he said. "He was a good man. But you need to watch your mouth and show some goddam respect, Barbara." He went back behind his desk.

"This friend of mine, his name is Billy DeSantis. He's coming in from Miami, or someplace in Florida, and he's bringing a very important package for me. I already told you everything you need to know and everything I want you to do. Just make sure he has a good time and that he doesn't think anything's been prearranged." He paused. "You understand what I'm saying, right?"

"I understand."

"Like I said, you're smart. Be smart about this." He handed her a thick envelope, and then turned his back on her. "This should help with any bullshit ethical concerns you may have."

The office of the Diocese of Brooklyn was in a prewar four-story orange brick building near Prospect Park. The building sat adjacent to Green-Wood Cemetery. Joshua exited the rental Kia he'd secured that morning, pushed six quarters into a parking meter, and walked inside.

The diocese owned and occupied the whole building. John Telentino's office was on the top floor with a view of traffic on the Prospect Expressway. His assistant showed Josh into the bishop's office. Without ceremonial vestments, the bishop looked like an ordinary priest to Josh. He was thinner and about three inches shorter than Josh. His bright brown eyes and still-dark hair set off an open, clean-shaven face with an olive complexion. The bishop rose from behind his desk and extended his hand.

"I know who you are, Mr. Abrahams," John said. He smiled. "It's a pleasure to meet you again." Joshua began to say something, but the bishop continued. "Let me make this simple for you. I was attending seminary at Patrick Fenton when you and your brother were born. While I wasn't involved in the process that led to your placement, I was very pleased when you and, later on, Michael, were adopted."

"Does this mean you know who my biological parents are, or were?" Josh asked.

"Oh, I hope that's not why you're here," the bishop said. "Because regardless of what I know or don't know, I'm prohibited from communicating anything about your adoption. In my limited experience, reporters are generally curious, so I'm sure you've made inquiries over the years. All I can say from what I know about adoptions involving the Church—and my experience in that area is limited—is that the Church respects the privacy of birth parents and adoptive parents. Unless, that is, the Church is expressly released from any liability that may flow from such a revelation."

Josh sat down and took out his reporter's notebook. "It's okay, sir, that's not why I'm here," he said. "I came across the story and recognized . . . myself in the photo of Father Michael. I asked my editor if I could take a few days to find out what I could about him, the crime, the case, anything relevant."

The bishop took a chair opposite Josh, crossed his legs, wove his fingers together in his lap, and leaned in. "Ask me what you'd like, Mr. Abrahams. I'll tell you everything I possibly can."

Most of what Josh asked and the bishop answered mirrored the police report and what he'd learned from Father James. Father Michael had been walking to the bank with the deposit from the Easter Sunday collection when one or more people confronted him. He was knocked to the ground during the robbery. He hit his head, first on a steel hydrant, then on the concrete, and suffered severe blunt-force trauma. He was dead by the time first responders got to him.

"Excuse me, Father. Do I call you 'Father' or 'Your Grace' or . . ."

The bishop smiled. "You're a polite young man, Mr. Abrahams. Call me John. May I call you Joshua?"

"Thank you. It's Josh." The reporter's curiosity kicked in. The bank bag had to be the target, not the priest. The people who did this had to believe the bag would contain enough to make the grab worthwhile. It's possible, actually likely, that they never intended to kill him.

"I'm sorry, sir, but I'm not familiar with this neighborhood. Is it a high crime area?" Josh asked.

The bishop sat up straight. "Actually, it's quite the

opposite. It's mostly residential, stable, diverse—I'd say it's not, but I haven't lived here for several years, so . . ."

Josh hesitated, then said, "Did Father Michael have enemies? I mean, could he have been the target of this, or was it just about the bank deposit cash?"

Bishop John looked away for a moment, then smiled, clasped his hands together, and leaned back in, toward Josh. "No, Joshua, your brother had absolutely no enemies. He was a very kind, very special young man who I wish you could have known." He wasn't ready to share anything about his family's jewels with the reporter. Not yet anyway. "Certainly, there's no way of knowing but I have to believe these criminals, murderers, I guess, had reason to think there'd be a significant amount of money—cash—from the Easter collections."

Josh nodded, stood up, and extended his hand to John Telentino. "I hate to ask this, but are you related to Angelo—"

The bishop held up his hand but remained seated. "Angelo is my brother. We have almost no relationship and haven't since we were both young men. It's not a secret, and it's not a problem to ask." He hesitated for a moment, then continued. "There aren't many Telentino's left. His wife was killed in a car accident over ten years ago. He has a son, Angelo Jr., who is a few years younger than you are."

"Thanks so much for your time. May I call on you again?" Josh asked.

"Anytime," John said.

"Oh, by the way, when I first walked in, you told me you were happy to see me again. Again?"

The bishop stood up and smiled. He put his arm around Josh's shoulders. "When you were about three days old, a few weeks before you were sent home with your parents, I met both you and Michael in the nursery." The bishop's eyes went somewhere for a moment. "As I recall, he was the quiet one."

Josh got into his rental car, programmed the GPS to take him back to the Hampton Inn, and slipped into afternoon traffic. He didn't register the black CTS following three cars behind him.

Before he caught the train from Miami to New York City, Billy DeSantis reached out one last time to Milos. The carrot Billy dangled was that he would, within two, maybe three days at most, pay off everything he owed. Milos gave Billy a referral in Chinatown. For a princely fee, this contact would provide everything he'd requested along with specific instructions. Milos restated his expectation that Billy would pay the entire debt, plus interest, in cash.

Billy bought a round-trip ticket with an open return on Amtrak's Silver Meteor from Miami. It was scheduled to arrive in plenty of time for him to take advantage of Angelo's hospitality. This was ironic because he planned to end his relationship with this particular client and, in so doing, ensure his own survival and future prosperity.

To Billy, the plan seemed bulletproof. With what he knew about the crime boss, and with what he was facing if he wasn't successful, the fact he was getting ready to do things he'd never before even thought of doing didn't cloud his mind.

The twenty-seven-hour trip from Miami to Penn Station was boring. It always was. Billy arrived in the afternoon and took a cab to Pell Street in Chinatown. In the back room of a quiet tailoring shop, he quickly completed his expensive business with an old woman who didn't utter a single word while he was there. He caught another cab uptown to the Sherry-Netherland. He checked in, went to his room, and used the in-room technology to identify some possible late-night companionship. After he'd collected a few interesting prospects, he took a shower, changed clothes, and headed down to Cipriani for dinner, compliments of the boss of the Telentino-Calabrese crime organization.

# CHAPTER 5

Angelo Jr. answered his mobile phone. "What do you need, Dominic?"

"It's hard to watch both of them by myself, Angelo," Dominic said. "The kid's been holed up except for going to morning Mass over at St. Brendan's. The girl takes off, comes back, and takes off again, like that. I don't know where she's going or what she's doing. I can't follow one of them without losing track of the other one. Maybe we should get another set of eyes?"

"Maybe you should do what the fuck you're told, okay?" Junior said.

"You got it, boss. Sorry, I was just thinking—"

"Don't think, Dominic. It's not your strong suit."

Angelo arranged help for Dominic so they could keep tabs on both Barbara and Bobby. The help would start the following afternoon.

❖

Barbara arrived at Cipriani at 7:30 p.m. wearing a short, tight-fitting black dress. She pointed to an empty table as perfect for the task at hand. Mr. T told her where Billy DeSantis was going to be seated, so where she placed herself would allow him to see enough to pique his interest.

DeSantis arrived a few minutes later and ordered a Bellini as soon as he sat down.

*Not awful*, she thought. He was maybe in his late forties, tall, dark hair and eyes, and nice white teeth. He was in lightweight gray slacks, a white open-collar silk shirt, and expensive black loafers. He had a thick gold chain around his neck. No socks. His look was very Italian and very Florida. But, just in case looks turned out to be deceiving, she had brought some crushed up MDMA she'd gotten from a girlfriend who tended bar at a strip club. If things got at all uncomfortable, the guy wouldn't know what hit him.

Barbara saw him immediately spot her. She sipped her Citrus Mist and checked her watch every minute or so. The waiter brought over a second drink and indicated Billy as her admirer. *This guy has the patience of a fruit fly*, she thought. She smiled at the waiter and then shot a dazzler in Billy's direction. He pantomimed asking if he could join her, but she mouthed *I'm waiting for someone, sorry, but thank you*, and raised her drink at him. Billy feigned a blow to his heart but smiled back.

The waiter brought Billy his appetizer. He dove into a steak tartare, noticed her looking at him, and pantomimed offering her a share. She smiled again and politely demurred, but the hook was set. As soon as he got his entrée, she accepted his invitation and began her assignment.

Billy finished his veal chop and orzo pasta while Barbara downed a spinach salad with walnuts, ricotta cheese, and bacon. Harry's red wine vinegar dressing was a feast in itself. They got along famously. Barbara resisted the impulse to believe she might enjoy this. She was on a long dry spell. But this was work; it was well compensated, but it was work, nothing else.

Billy made his move after they split a dessert of crepes and vanilla ice cream. "You know, I'm surprised, but I can't say I'm disappointed your date didn't show up," he said, dabbing at the corners of his mouth. She couldn't yet determine if his complexion was naturally olive-toned or tanned from the south Florida sun. She leaned in. For Billy, the view she presented would be exceptional.

"Actually, neither am I," she said. "I'll tell you this, I don't plan on giving him a second chance."

Billy stood up and pulled Barbara's chair out for her. She smiled and walked in front of him to the lobby elevators. She knew he'd follow, but not too close.

The Sherry featured plush hotel rooms and suites on the lower floors. The upper floors were apartments for wealthy New Yorkers or businesses needing hotel amenities along with an upscale midtown residential address. Billy had a suite on the eleventh floor. It had set Angelo back $1,600 for the two nights he was scheduled to be in the city.

"Wow," she said. "This isn't a bad place to stay when you visit the city."

Billy was on her immediately. He grabbed her breasts from behind and rubbed himself against her. "Whoa, big guy," she said, twisting from his grasp. "At least offer a girl a drink?"

She sat in a wingback chair directly across from a large flat-screen television disguised as a mirror. She crossed her legs slowly.

"Yeah, sorry," he said, heading for a bar stocked with Angelo's preferences. "What would the lady like?"

"Why don't we open that red over there," she said, pointing to a diamond shaped display with four bottles of Sangiovese from the Umbria region.

"You have good taste," he said. "And I'll bet you taste good too."

*Another classless piece of shit*, she thought, happy now to have brought the ketamine-laced ecstasy. He poured them each a glass of wine, and they both took a taste. Then, as she hoped he would, he moved toward the bathroom.

"Why don't we meet inside," he said, pointing to the bedroom. He disappeared behind the bathroom door.

She stood and smiled, dosed his drink, and slipped out of her dress but stayed in the living room. He stepped out of the bathroom wearing just a pair of baby blue boxers.

"Jesus," he said when he saw her lying on the sofa. Barbara had that effect on men when she was dressed or, in this case, undressed to impress. She raised her glass. In a single gulp, he downed his whole drink. They grappled on the sofa for about a minute before she led him toward the bedroom. Billy got very excited just before he slipped into a deep sleep.

Barbara dressed immediately. She messed up the bed, making sure it carried her scent. She took a pair of panties out of her purse. She removed the ones she was wearing and threw them on the floor. She went through his wallet and grabbed one of his business cards. Fort Lauderdale, not Miami. She looked around for a suitcase or a computer. There was nothing, just a gym bag. That was odd.

When he woke up he'd find a note from her thanking him for a very good time, with a lipstick print next to the "B" she would sign. She took pains to keep anything personal or professional to herself. She didn't recall him even asking her name. After half an hour she quietly slipped out the door and rode the elevator to the lobby. She stopped at Harry's bar for a nightcap before taking a cab home to Brooklyn.

❖

Early the next morning Junior banged on the apartment door. When Barbara answered he pushed his way in.

"Where's your fucking brother?" he said.

"Obviously he's not here, asshole," she said, pointing to the couch where her brother typically slept. He slapped her hard across the cheek.

"You need to learn some fucking respect, Barbara," he said.

Without missing a beat, she kicked him, hard, in the balls. "You need to get the fuck out of my place before I have a conversation with your daddy, *Junior. Capisce?*"

He looked hard at her, his eyes watering. "Your day is gonna come, bitch. You tell your brother I was here and that I need to see him."

"You stay the hell away from him, Angelo. I mean it," she said in a voice as tough as she could muster. She didn't want to let him know what she knew. Not yet. "You have nothing he needs, and he damn sure doesn't have anything for you."

Junior walked out of her apartment and slammed the door behind him. Bobby came out from where he'd been hiding in Barbara's closet.

"He's gone," she said, placing her hands on his shoulders. "He is very bad news, Bobby. The only thing keeping him in line at all is his asshole father."

She wished she could rat the bastard out to the police for what had happened with Father Mike. But she couldn't, not without implicating her brother. Besides, in this community, and for these people, the police weren't exactly friends.

Josh caught up on his notes and did a little online research on Bishop John Telentino. He already knew the bishop's brother ran a criminal enterprise he'd inherited from his uncle. He knew that John Telentino had also attended Patrick Fenton but moved on to Notre Dame to finish his doctorate at their prestigious divinity school.

After ordination, he returned to Brooklyn to help lead the faith community at St. Brendan's. A dozen years later, he'd been elevated to bishop of the diocese and handed the neighborhood church back to his friend and mentor, Father James Wakely. Around three years after he became bishop, he arranged for a young Father Michael Olivetti to be assigned to St. Brendan's when he'd finished up at Patrick Fenton.

Billy DeSantis rolled out of bed with a 24-karat headache. It took a few minutes, four Tylenol, and two cups of strong black coffee for him to shake loose the cobwebs and recall the previous night. There were two empty Sangiovese bottles in the living room and another in the bedroom. He looked around and noticed the panties. He smiled, picked them up, and rubbed them over his face. He read her note, saw the lip print, and nodded his head. He didn't remember much, but he convinced himself he'd had a really good time. After a long hot shower, he dressed and went down to the lobby for breakfast.

When he finished, he took a waiting cab to Penn Station. He retrieved two briefcases from a locker and replaced them with the gym bag he'd brought to the hotel. He called John Telentino and told him he would be at the diocesan office in a half hour.

Billy's meeting with the bishop lasted forty minutes. They talked a bit about family and briefly about the unfortunate events involving Father Michael. Billy got no sense as to why the bishop needed $250,000 in cash, but that wasn't his concern. John's account was decent, but nothing compared to Angelo's.

Billy caught another cab into the city, this time to the Marriott Courtyard at E. 40th Street and 5th Avenue. He and Milos had discussed ways for Billy to cover his tracks in the event that things went sideways later on. He sat at a table against the wall in a far corner of the quiet lobby. He opened the remaining briefcase. It contained $250,000 in cash and a small black leather zippered case. Inside the case were two syringes filled with a chemical mixture Milos assured him would do exactly what Billy needed done. Billy was in uncharted waters, but he knew Milos had a vested interest in his success, so he trusted the Chinatown connection.

From previous visits, Billy believed he knew how the evening with Angelo would play out. The briefcase would stay in the car and Angelo's driver would pat Billy down before dinner. Billy made sure to have something for the driver to find.

Once back in the car, after dessert at Ferrara's, Angelo would begin to doze on the way to a private uptown club where they'd usually enjoy the company of some skilled, expensive Korean masseuses. When the fun was over, Angelo's driver would drop Billy at the Sherry, and Angelo would head back to Brooklyn.

That's the way his visits had gone on Billy's three most recent trips to see Angelo Telentino Sr. His last visit, around six months earlier, had required two duffels to carry nearly $800,000 in cash that Angelo needed to run through Billy's investment laundry.

Not this time, though. This time the agenda was Billy's, not Angelo's.

At six, Billy walked into the bar at the Sherry and ordered a Bellini. He checked out the restaurant just in case the hottie from the previous evening happened to be there. Had he even gotten her name? Clearly it was something with a *B*. He couldn't remember. He finished his drink and stepped outside. He waited less than ten minutes. A black Escalade pulled up. The backseat window rolled down.

"Billy D.," Angelo said, smiling. "Get in. We got a table at La Luna."

# CHAPTER 6

Junior reached out to Mikey DeMartini. Mikey was keeping tabs on Bobby Quattrone while Dominic focused on Barbara's comings and goings. In Junior's mind, if Dominic Ciccone was dumb as a stump, Mikey was the stump.

"Hey, Mikey, I need you to do something for me. There's half a C-note in it for you."

"Can you make it fifty, Angelo? I need some new underwear."

"For you, Mikey, I can do that."

"You're the best, man," Mikey said. "What do you need?"

"You know the Hampton Inn in Sheepshead Bay?"

"Yeah, I think so," Mikey said. "It's a hotel, right?"

Junior looked at the phone and shook his head. "That's right, Mikey," he said. "It's a hotel. Here's what I need you to do."

❖

The ride to La Luna was full of how's-the-family questions and answers. Angelo was in an expansive mood. He talked a lot about a lot of things. Billy just listened and smiled. He'd learned from his own father, Pete DeSantis, that the job was to take the client's cash, invest it conservatively, and avoid discussion of anything that might become a legal issue down the road. "Smile and nod, Billy," Pete had told his son. "These guys are not our friends."

When they got to Mulberry Street, Angelo's driver, Carmine, put a hand up and stopped Billy from entering the restaurant, as expected.

"Sorry, Mr. DeSantis," he said, beginning his frisk.

"No problem," Billy said. "There's a—yeah, right there." Carmine found the nine-millimeter handgun Billy was licensed to carry. "All this cash, you know."

"I'll just hold it until later, sir," Carmine said, stopping his frisk before his hands went any place else that could have caused Billy a problem.

Billy had taped a syringe to the inside of each thigh, uncovered, needle down. He knew there was some serious danger to this, but he also knew this was the best way for him to play out his plan. He'd cut away both his pants pockets so he could easily reach the syringes when they were needed. He'd get the $200 pair of trousers fixed when he returned to Florida.

There were a few tables occupied on the right side of the tile-floored dining room but nothing on the left. There was a lonely table behind a room divider with a small, folded card marked "Reserved." On top of the stiff white tablecloth sat an open bottle of Chianti, two filled glasses, and a small burner under an aromatic pot of mussels bubbling in a sauce thick with garlic, butter, and olive oil. Billy took a deep breath; the aroma was intoxicating. A tiny woman wearing a long white apron lit the burner.

"Good evening, Mr. T," she said, offering a cheek for him to kiss.

"Mama Luna!" He smiled, bent down, and kissed first her left and then her right cheek. "Meet my friend Billy. He's in from Florida." She nodded.

"That smells wonderful," Billy said, smiling at the woman.

She smiled back at him and nodded again. "We've got some very nice veal tonight," she said, addressing Angelo. "Nunzio is making some osso buco for you and your friend. And he's got fresh homemade linguini too. You'll do dessert down the street?"

"Too soon to talk about dessert, Mama," Angelo said. He took a seat with his back to the wall. He pointed Billy to a seat backing up to the front window. Mama Luna smiled, bowed, and left.

"I appreciate you coming up, Billy," he said. "Did you bring a statement with you, like I asked?"

"Yes sir, everything's in the case, but before I left, I mailed you one," Billy said. "I'll go over the one I brought with me when we're on the way back to the Sherry."

"No rush," Angelo said. "After dinner, if we can still walk, we'll get some cake at Ferarra's and then we'll see. I know this place uptown."

The two of them went through the full pot of mussels, a robust antipasto, two bottles of Chianti, and maybe the best veal Billy had ever eaten, including the grilled chop he'd had the evening before at the Sherry. They shared a dry after-dinner M&R Vermouth and talked about Billy's father and Angelo's son but nothing of Angelo's business or of his brother, the bishop.

"I don't know, Billy," Angelo said. "You followed in your father's footsteps and didn't miss a beat. Still doing the job and still pushing out good returns."

"Thank you, Angelo. I do my best."

"Junior's another story, though," he said. "I give him a lot of room, you know? I don't try to force anything on him, but he—I don't know. He got too much of his mother in him. He's not made of the same kind of stuff as me."

"Who is?" Billy asked. "There aren't too many like you left."

"That's probably a good thing," Angelo said with a short laugh. "I don't know what to do with him."

"Maybe he's not cut out for your thing, you know?"

"He thinks he is, though, and that's what worries me," Angelo said. "Sometimes I think I should leave him out of this entirely, but he really wants to make his mark."

Billy pushed himself away from the table. "Sometimes people have to find their own way, Angelo," he said. "Take me. I'm always looking for new opportunities, you know?"

Angelo signaled for the check, knowing there wouldn't be one. "All I can tell you, when all's said and done, is that however it plays out, he's gonna be lost. Those other guys? They'll eat him alive."

The sun eased down and out of the evening sky. Dusk descended, and after a slow walk up the street and a plateful of pastries at Ferarra's, Angelo asked Billy if he wanted an Espresso. Billy declined, saying it would keep him up all night. Angelo nodded and followed suit. They returned to the back seat of the Escalade. Billy leaned back, content in the knowledge that it wouldn't be five minutes before Angelo began to doze on the trip uptown.

Carmine followed Canal Street west before turning right, onto 6th Avenue. He drove through lower Manhattan, heading toward the Upper West Side. Angelo snored while Billy watched the city's streets go by.

Billy both liked and disliked New York. He'd probably spend more time in the city if he could turn that little tomato he played with last night into a steady thing. *She was a hot number*, he thought. *Italian, too.*

The Escalade came to a stop at a red light behind

two taxis at W. 31st Street and 6th Avenue. Billy slipped his right hand into his pocket and peeled a single strip of tape off the syringe on his thigh. He kept his eyes on Carmine, carefully brought the needle out, and in a single swift motion stuck it into Angelo's left forearm and hit the plunger. The boss barely moved. In less than a minute his head slumped onto his right shoulder.

When he'd emptied the entire load, Billy dropped the syringe onto the mat between his feet and used his left shoe to slide it just under the front seat. Carmine eased the SUV back into uptown traffic.

At W. 37th Street and 6th Avenue the curtain rose on act two of Billy's little play. He leaned across the seat and tried to rouse Angelo, but the paralytic had done its job. Angelo Telentino was on his way to whatever fresh hell would have him.

"Carmine! Hey, Carmine," Billy said, forcing some alarm into his voice. "I think something's wrong with Angelo!" he said, shaking the arm he'd shot the poison into. "Come on, Angelo! Wake up!"

Angelo's driver turned onto W. 40th Street and pulled into a spot on the left side of the street in front of a small office building near the middle of the block. After Carmine jumped out of the driver's seat, Billy got out. He encouraged Carmine to check on Angelo from where he'd just exited the SUV. Carmine leaned into the back seat and attempted to rouse his boss.

Billy peeled the second syringe off his thigh, slipped the needle into Carmine's calf, pushed the big man down, and closed the door. By the time Billy made it to the other side of the car, Carmine was slack-jawed and glassy-eyed, unable to go for his weapon. Billy collected the first syringe and grabbed the valise with the cash. He pulled the gun the bodyguard had appropriated from him earlier from Carmine's jacket pocket. He slammed the Escalade's door and walked at a leisurely pace back to 6th Avenue.

Billy was exhilarated. He'd put two made men down, one of them a New York City family boss, and he wasn't even breathing hard.

In his Sheepshead Bay hotel room, Josh awoke early the next morning to news of a bizarre discovery over-night in New York's garment district. Two men were found dead in the back seat of a late-model black Cadillac Escalade.

"Sources tell New York One that one of the dead has been identified as Angelo Telentino, the fifty-eight-year-old leader of Brooklyn's notorious Calabrese crime family," said anchor Pat Sullivan. "Early indi-cations are that he was the victim of a well-planned execution; however, the actual cause of death will not be confirmed until an autopsy is performed by the New York County medical examiner."

Joshua stared at the screen. The scene on the TV revealed at least six marked cruisers, a handful of unmarked police vehicles, yards of yellow tape, a black SUV, and a whole array of flashing lights. Under the live video, the crawl superimposed the words *CRIME BOSS KILLED ON THE STREETS OF THE CITY.*

"The second body in the back seat of the late-model Cadillac Escalade has now been identified as that of Carmine Calabrese," Sullivan reported. "He was said to be Telentino's nephew, driver, and bodyguard. Like his boss, there's no word as of now on cause of death. Inquiries have been referred to Telentino's brother, Bishop John Telentino of the Brooklyn Roman Catholic Diocese. Unfortunately, the bishop learned of his brother's death from media calls in the middle of the night and understandably has had no comment."

Josh called the diocesan office and was told the bishop wouldn't be in until much later, if at all, due to a death in his immediate family. Then Josh called his paper and filled in Jasper, his editor.

"I don't know if these murders are linked," Josh said, "but there is connective tissue between the young priest and the older crime boss."

"Yeah," Jasper said. "The bishop, right?"

"That's right," Josh said.

"Take all the time you need. This is juicy stuff."

"I'll be in touch," Josh said.

Josh took the elevator down and exited the hotel lobby into the small parking lot. He saw his rented Kia was listing to one side. Both tires on the driver's side of the car had been slashed. "Damn," he said. "Well, that kind of sucks."

"Sure does, pal," said a guy walking into the hotel. "Welcome to Brooklyn."

Josh noticed a message scratched into the hood of the car: *mind your fucking business, asshole.* Josh called the rental car company, told them what had happened, and waited in the parking lot for them to bring him a new car.

The taxi stopped at the corner of Elm Avenue and E. 12th Street. Bishop Telentino was in street clothes: khaki slacks, a blue button-down Oxford shirt, and oxblood loafers. He got out of the cab, walked down past Avenue N, crossed the street, and came to a stop in front of a house in the middle of the block. He casually surveyed his surroundings. Satisfied that no one was watching, he walked up the three steps to the front door, inserted a key into a lower lock, then another into a deadbolt.

Inside, he took the stairs to the second level, opened a door, and continued up another staircase. A door at the end of a short hallway opened into a large airy chamber. There was a bathroom to the left, a closet on the right, a small flat-screen television on the back wall, and a large, canopied bed on the other side of the doorway. A middle-aged woman sat quietly in an antique Queen Anne chair in front of a curtained window. The view included the place on E. 12th Street where, days earlier, Father Mike had been robbed and killed by two young men wearing masks as she watched in horror.

The TV was on NY1. The sound was turned off and the closed captioning was turned on.

She walked over to the bishop, knelt, and kissed his hand. He took her face in his hands, kissed her on each cheek, and hugged her.

"Are you all right?" he said aloud as he signed to her. She nodded. "Do you want to come downstairs to the kitchen, perhaps?"

She shook her head and motioned for him to sit in an armchair across from the one she had been sitting in.

"Do you have everything you need?" he said.

She nodded and signed, "Would you like something to drink?"

"No, thank you. Is there anything more you can remember?"

She shook her head. He looked deeply into her eyes. She put her hands onto the arms of the chair.

"My brother . . ." She stiffened but held onto the chair. "My brother is dead," he said. "He was murdered last night."

She nodded once and pointed to the TV. "Are you okay?" she signed.

"Yes, I am. I wanted you to know."

"It's okay," she signed. "I'm okay." She smiled at him. "I'm sorry."

He shook his head. "Nothing to be sorry for. There was nothing left between us." He got up. She followed him to the doorway but stayed inside the room.

He signed, "Someday soon, you'll come out from this room and out from this house, and you'll never worry again about anything."

"I don't know," she signed.

"I do," he signed back. "I promise. *Ti amo*, Violetta. I will always take care of you." He squeezed her hands and kissed her cheek. He walked down the stairs and out the front door.

In the years since he was first ordained and after he returned to Brooklyn, John Telentino had taken advantage of an unwanted inheritance from his father, delivered through his uncle. He'd purchased several distressed properties near Catholic churches throughout Brooklyn, and after rehabilitating them, they'd served as refuge for people who temporarily needed a safe place. Abuse victims, homeless mothers and children, and even a few petty criminals John felt didn't belong in the prison system. In most of the houses, the people who stayed there came and went. In this house, Violetta Mazzarese had lived a safe, albeit reclusive existence since returning to Brooklyn from St. Louis three years after John was ordained.

Only he and Father Michael had tended to her needs. One or the other prayed with her, offered her communion, bought and delivered groceries, fixed things that needed attention in the house, and sometimes just visited with her.

John recalled the day, six years earlier, when Michael had come to his office unannounced.

# May 2010

"Is Violetta my mother?" Father Michael said.

All the bishop could do was smile. "How did you figure that out?"

"That's not the question," the young priest said.

John tilted his head quizzically.

"The question is, does she know?" Michael said.

The bishop stood and walked around his desk. He sat in the chair next to Michael. "What do you think?"

"I think she's known since the day you brought me to see her," Michael said.

The two men sat silently for a full minute. John grappled with how much to tell the young man. Noise from traffic on the Prospect Expressway filtered in through the open window behind the bishop's desk.

"What makes you say that?" the bishop asked.

"Are we doing the whole Socratic thing?"

John laughed out loud. "You've learned much, grasshopper," he said. "Yes, she's known for a while, not the first day, but a while, and I'm sure it's been difficult for her to not smother you with love whenever you visit her."

The young priest rose, put his hands on the back of his chair, and smiled down at the man who'd been his sponsor, mentor, and father figure.

"I don't want to upset anything, Bishop," he said. "But I'd like to be able to be a son to my mother. I was crushed when my adoptive mother died, but now it seems like there could be a second chance." He looked to the heavens. "I understand why these things are so complicated."

"They are," the bishop said. Michael knew nothing about his biological father, but nothing could be gained by burdening a young priest with that kind of baggage. *Still* . . . "You haven't told me how you came to gain this particular nugget of wisdom," the bishop said.

"I was visiting with her and noticed my own reflection in the mirror behind where she was sitting. It was a case of almost immediately recognizing yourself in someone else. If I ever meet my brother, I'm sure it will feel something like this."

John laughed again. "If you ever meet your brother, you'll figure it out much quicker than, what did this take, nearly six years?"

John stood and opened the door to his office. "Nancy," he said to his secretary, "would you please cancel the rest of my day for me?"

"Certainly, sir," she said.

He turned to Father Michael. "Well, are you coming?" He smiled. The two of them left to visit the woman they both had come to cherish.

## October 2016

Under the circumstances, John thought Violetta was handling what had happened to Michael as well as could possibly be expected. Surviving the kind of trauma-filled existence she'd experienced might make it seem to others that she could absorb even enormous body blows. How many more like this she could take, though, was hard even for a man of powerful faith like the bishop of Brooklyn to consider.

# CHAPTER 7

Billy didn't sleep on the return trip to Miami, but he relaxed a little after the train passed through Washington, DC. He started planning his future somewhere in North Carolina. He convinced himself that the plan had gone off without a hitch. He had increased his net worth by the quarter-million in cash inside the case plus another $13 million currently sitting in Angelo's investment account. He would redirect those funds carefully, intermittently, beginning a few weeks after he got back to south Florida.

First, though, he had to settle up with Milos.

Junior was seated behind his father's desk trying to get a sense of how the world appeared from that chair. He had choices before him, decisions to make. With his father gone, he could either buddy up to Joey Sitriani, Angelo's unquestioned number two, or he could try to make an end run around Sitriani and take control of the family himself. Even at nearly thirty, he'd be considered too young and inexperienced to run one of New York's most entrenched and ruthless crime families. On the other hand, if he moved fast enough and hard enough, no one would see him coming.

His old man wasn't yet in the ground, so he had time to think and to plan. Grieve? Yeah, maybe a little, for show. First, he needed to see what, if any, surprises were living inside his father's desk. Second, he'd do whatever he needed to do to collect what was coming to him from his uncle, the bishop. Then, he'd take care of Barbara Quattrone's stupid-as-shit brother, the only one who could tie him to Father Mike's death.

Barbara also had decisions to make. She knew Junior was off his father's leash and would be anxious to settle scores. She left the jewels where Bobby had put them and, out of concern for her brother, hadn't yet called the police. She decided on another course of action.

Her van was in the shop, so she got out of the subway at Prospect Park and walked to the diocesan office. When she opened the door to the anteroom outside the bishop's private office, she bumped into Josh Abrahams.

"We meet again," he said, standing.

"We do. Interesting morning," she said. "Listen, I'm sorry about the other day . . . What did you say your name was?"

"Josh," he said

"Joshua, right. I'm a little off my game right now. I guess you're waiting for Bishop Telentino, right? I know, stupid question."

She sat down diagonally across from him. She caught him trying not to stare and smoothed her tight jeans, rethinking the red heels and snug red scoop-neck top she had chosen that morning.

"I'm sorry," he said. "Did you tell me your name after Father Mike's funeral?"

She smiled. "Probably not," she said, leaning in and extending a hand with long red polished nails and rings on three fingers. "Barbara Quattrone."

The bishop entered his small suite of offices. He smiled at the two of them. "On another day, I might comment on what a nice-looking couple you two make," he said, "but I'm not feeling especially chatty right now."

"I'm sorry about your brother," Josh said. The bishop thanked him and nodded.

"I know you were already here," Barbara said to Josh, "but can I talk to Bishop first? I promise I won't be long."

"Sure," Josh said, "but only if I can buy you a bite of lunch after we're both done?"

She looked straight into his eyes. There was something there. "Yeah, absolutely," she said. "Lunch would be good."

She followed the bishop into his office and closed

the door. About ten minutes passed before the office door opened and she walked out.

"You're up," she said. "I'll wait here."

The bishop looked out his window at the cars racing by on the elevated expressway. Josh closed the door.

"Sir, do you think these two crimes are connected in any way?"

John turned around and looked at him for a few seconds. "I suppose I'm a common denominator," he said, "but even that thread is pretty slender. No, without more information, I don't see how what happened to Father Mike and what happened to my brother last night are connected, but, really, who knows? Right now, Joshua, I'm not sure of very much."

"In the business he was in, your brother could have been taken down by any number of people," Josh said.

"That's true," John said. "As I told you, in no way were we remotely close."

Josh sat down. "I just want to express my condolences, sir. Even though you two were estranged, it still has to hurt, I mean, on top of losing Father Michael. Is there anything new you can tell me about that? I talked twice to Detective Otis. The police are doing a lot of running, but mostly in circles, and I'm sure they're going to be a whole lot busier now, with your brother's murder."

John exhaled a breath he'd been holding. "Can we speak completely off the record, Joshua?"

Josh slid his notebook into his back pocket. "Of

course, John. You know I have more than just a reporter's interest here. But at some point, I hope we can go on the record."

The bishop stood, walked around his desk, and sat down in the chair next to Josh's.

"Two things," John said. "First, let me tell you what was really stolen in the robbery.

"My mother's name was Maria Conti Telentino. She passed over thirty-two years ago. I was in the apartment that day with her and the young girl who came over from Italy to help care for her. My mother was bedridden and in the final stages of pancreatic cancer. She wanted to die at home. It looked like it might be soon, so I called my Uncle Vito to get Angelo to come home.

"Before he got there, she told me about the trust funds our uncle had set up. They were substantial, almost three-quarters of a million dollars for each of us. They'd been placed with a close family friend who assisted Uncle Vito and some others in their business with matters such as this.

"Soon before Angelo got there, she told me to go into a bureau and pull out a pouch hidden in the back of one of the drawers. As always, at least where she was concerned, I did what I was told. Inside were two long strands of what looked for all the world like huge chunks of cut glass in different colors, held together by thick dark brown metal wire. To tell you the truth, Josh, they looked to my young eyes like a bunch of junk."

"That was what the thief was after in the shopping bag Father James talked to me about, right?" Josh asked.

The bishop nodded. "She told me to hide the jewels in my room and not to let my brother get his hands on them. She said they'd been in her family since the fifteenth century. She told me they could be worth a fortune. Or they could be worth nothing. I still don't know about any of that, but they belong in the family. She told me to keep them, trusting I'd do what's right.

"She died about half an hour after Angelo got there." He stopped talking for a moment, shaking his head and wiping at his eyes.

"I kept the jewels, as she'd asked. After I was ordained and came home, I loaned them to St. Brendan's. Every Easter and every Christmas we adorn the statue of the Virgin in the vestibule at the front of the church. Then, after those holy days, we put them back into a safe deposit box I keep in the bank up on Avenue M. That's where Michael was going when he was robbed. It wasn't about the collection; it was about the jewels."

"That explains the attack," Josh said. "Whoever did this must have known what was in that bag and wanted the jewels. He was probably at Easter service, and he probably knew where and when they'd be returned to the bank deposit box."

"The police didn't release anything about the jewels to the media," John said. "The day after . . . I can't believe it's only been less than a week, and so much has happened. The day after, Father James got a ransom call for $250,000."

He walked behind his desk, opened a drawer, took out a gym bag, and put it on the desk. "That's $250,000," he said. "I'm waiting for a call, either from the person who did this or from Father James."

Josh started to pace. "You can't handle this by yourself, sir. First, it's not safe, but second, Father Mike is dead. Your brother, who understood this kind of stuff, is dead. You really should let the police know what's going on."

"I'm not going to do anything dangerous," John said. "I made a promise to my mother, and I can't renege on that. But there's more."

"I know you have something else to share, sir, but would you mind telling me something, anything about Father Mike?" Josh asked.

John removed his eyeglasses, closed his eyes, and gently massaged the bridge of his nose. He replaced his glasses and leaned in. "Your brother was special, Joshua," he said. "As soon as I could, after I was elevated to my present post, I sent for him. He was supporting an established congregation in southern Illinois, Carbondale, near where his adoptive parents used to live in Alton."

Josh nodded. "I recall Father James telling me Michael didn't have any living relatives—that he knew of, of course."

"That's true," the bishop said. "His adoptive parents

are both gone. After he lost his mother, he reached out to the Mother Superior at Patrick Fenton. She let me know they'd offered to take Michael in and asked if I'd give him a call."

"How old was he when she died?" Josh asked.

"He was thirteen," John said. "He was just becoming a young man."

Josh sat patiently, hoping Barbara hadn't lost interest. "Had to be tough," he said, "moving into a seminary, for an otherwise normal thirteen-year-old kid."

"Teenage boys are extremely hard to place into adoption," John said. "I told him he'd be able to attend school outside of the seminary and, when he was old enough, would be able to drive and to come and go as he pleased." He hesitated and smiled. "Okay, maybe not as he pleased, but as long as he respected the environment and Mother Superior's rules, he'd be fine."

"What kind of kid was he?" Josh asked.

"As far as I could glean from a thousand miles away, a pretty normal kid, a good kid."

Joshua smiled. "So was I, I guess. That said, I got to grow up an only child in a sort of, kind of Jewish household in a relatively normal suburban community outside the city of St. Louis."

"And until he found himself with no family to live with, Michael had a normal life, too," John said. "I wouldn't say I kept tabs, but I spoke to—I'm not really sure how much of this kind of information I should be sharing, especially with a reporter."

Josh cocked his head. "I'm not a reporter right now, sir," he said. "I'm just . . . a guy wondering about the brother I never got to know. Nothing you tell me seems connected to the story I'm writing about his murder. Unless you tell me something directly related to what happened on E. 12th Street, or what happened in Manhattan the other night, it's all just for me."

John tried to stifle a yawn but failed. Josh smiled. "I'm sorry for distracting you, sir. You said there were two things you wanted to tell me."

"You know, maybe we'll save number two for another time," he said, standing up. "You go have lunch with Barbara. Maybe . . ." Josh waited, but that was all he said. They shook hands. John looked Josh in the eyes. "Off the record, right?"

"Off the record, sir, for now. I may want to revisit some of this later on. I appreciate everything you've shared with me, and I promise to respect your confidence. Thank you."

The bishop's phone rang just as Josh and Barbara exited the outer office.

Josh drove his new rental, a Hyundai Sonata. Barbara navigated. They parked on Kings Highway near the corner of E. 12th Street. Josh fed the meter, and they went into a small sandwich shop on Quentin Road, just off Coney Island Avenue.

"My brother and I come here sometimes," Barbara said. "Food's good, there's plenty of it, and it's cheap. It's not fancy. I hope you don't mind."

Josh smiled at her. "I'm not here for the food," he said. "Just want to get to know you a little better."

"I, uh, I'm not at my best right now," she said, twisting a ring on her finger.

"Can't see how it could get much better." He smiled at her. "Are you okay?"

"What are you doing here?" she asked. She leaned back in her chair and stared at him. "You know, without all that hair on your face . . ."

He made a quick decision. "I know," he said. "I look like him, right?"

She cocked her head and stared some more. "Holy Mary, Mother of God. That's what my brother was talking about."

They ordered hero sandwiches and diet Cokes.

Josh couldn't decide whether she might be a source for his story or something else, but he felt comfortable with her. She was smart, curious, interesting, and so good looking. They sat for a few minutes, eating, and not talking. She must have been famished because he was only halfway done with his when she went up to the counter and bought chocolate chip cookies.

"I'm impressed, but I know you can't always eat like this," he said.

For the first time, she really smiled at him.

"I haven't eaten much of anything for a couple of days," she said. "I didn't realize how hungry I was. Sorry."

"No worries," he said. "Gotta love a woman with a healthy appetite."

She pushed a cookie at him. "So, he was your brother and you never met him?"

"I knew he existed," Josh said, "but I had no clue who adopted him, where he was living, anything, until his picture crossed my desk at the newspaper I work for in St. Louis. There was no mistaking him." He leaned back and went to speak but hesitated.

"What?" Barbara asked him.

"How long did you know Father Mike?"

She smiled. "Let me see. My brother is twenty-three, and if I'm remembering right, Michael arrived at St. Brendan's right around Bobby's confirmation—maybe eight, nine years ago?"

Josh let his eyes roam the restaurant, thinking. His gaze settled on a picture of an old Ferris wheel behind Barbara's head. She turned her head around to see what had captured his attention.

"That's the Wonder Wheel in Coney Island," she said. "Want to try it out?"

"It's still there?"

"You're surprised?"

"It just looks, I don't know, old?"

He smiled at her. "Eight or nine years ago you say.

That would have made him about twenty-four. Did you know him well? Oh," he put his hands up, "I don't mean—"

She laughed. "I know what you mean, and I know what you don't mean," she said. "He was always nice and respectful to me, but Bobby . . . Bobby didn't have a real man in his life back then. My father wasn't around—not that he was any kind of role model."

"You know," he said, "some people think that when you're a separated twin you somehow . . . on some level you know it, and there's always this feeling . . . I don't know . . ."

"Like something's missing?"

He shook his head. "No, I never really felt that," Josh said. "When I was nine, my parents told me I was adopted and that there was a twin. I was just starting to play schoolyard basketball—"

"Father Mike played basketball," she said. "He got Bobby into it. They'd sometimes play with some kids—black kids—from the other side of the avenue." She pointed to her right, at Coney Island Avenue.

They continued eating their lunch.

"After he arrived at St. Brendan's, he got my brother involved more and more with the Church," she said.

"Was that a good thing?"

"Oh, yeah," she said. "Bobby became an alter server for a couple of years. Helped out with the little kids who attended school at St. Brendan's, kind of a teacher's aide."

"Sounds like he took to it," Josh said.

She nibbled at her lower lip for a moment, appearing distracted.

"Are you okay?" he asked.

She swallowed. "He was a very good influence on my brother," she said, shaking her head. "He was helping Bobby get more involved in the Church, and he encouraged him to get his college degree. Bobby might have finished school if he hadn't gotten involved with Junior." She looked at Josh. "I know you know this, but it really sucks, what happened to Father Mike."

Josh nodded. "Wish I could have met him, known him. I guess, on some level, that's part of why I'm here. I appreciate you talking to me about him."

She finished off the rest of her drink, leaned back in her seat, and stretched.

*God,* Josh thought, *that right there is one fine-looking woman!*

"So, Mr. Abrahams," she said, a sly smile returning to her face, "is there a Mrs. Abrahams or a wannabe Mrs. Abrahams waiting patiently for you back in St. Louis?"

Josh couldn't keep his own smile from creeping onto his face. He leaned in and looked from side to side. He gestured for her to come close. Barbara put her face less than an inch from his. He moved slightly to his right and leaned in further, ending up right next to her left ear.

"My mom," he whispered. "She's Mrs. Abrahams."

She didn't miss a beat. "The only one?"

"For now," he said. "And no, there's no one in the batter's box."

They stared into each other's eyes. Josh wanted to shift the conversation. "What's your connection to all of these people? I'm sorry," he said before she could answer. "I'm a reporter. I ask questions. You don't have to—"

She put her hand over his. It was warm, dry. "You can ask me anything you want," she said. Then, softly, "I'm not sure why, but it feels good having someone to talk to."

# CHAPTER 8

On the third ring, Billy DeSantis answered with his name.

"This is Angelo Telentino. Do I know you?"

Billy paused. "You don't sound like Angelo. Wait, is this Angelo Jr.?" he asked after regaining his composure.

"Yeah, it is. Who are you?"

"I know your father. He's a, well, he was a client of mine."

"So, you know?"

"Know what?" Billy asked. "I haven't spoken to Angelo in, let me think, eight months. He called last year, in the fall, to clean out his account with my firm."

"My father is dead," Junior said. "They found him and my cousin Carmine in the city. What kind of account does he have?"

Billy considered his options. "I'm sorry to hear that, Angelo," he said. "I had no idea."

"I asked you what kind of account he has," Junior said.

"Had," Billy said. "Like I told you, last September, or October . . . wait a second." He made some noise opening and closing a drawer. "Last October he called and closed the account. I brought him the cash, and that's the last time we spoke. He's really dead?"

"Why do I have to repeat stuff? Yeah, he's dead. Somebody killed him and Carmine last night. Don't you get news where you live? Where are you, anyway?"

Billy told Junior only that he was in Florida and repeated that his father used to engage his services but had closed his account with DeSantis Management.

"What did you *manage* for my father?" Junior asked.

"You know, Angelo," Bill said, "I'm not really comfortable discussing this with you. There's no relationship any longer and my business with your father was between him and me. I'm really very sorry for your loss." He hung up.

The bishop answered the call put through by his secretary.

"Yes?"

"Listen," a voice said. "Don't talk. Just listen. Bring the money—"

"Who is this?"

"This is who's got your stuff, and this is who's giving you an hour to get to the northeast corner of Kings

Highway and Coney Island Avenue with the cash and then wait there for instructions." The line went dead.

John exited the taxi on the corner of Coney Island Avenue and Quentin Road, a block from where he was told to be. This was a busy part of the neighborhood, which was likely why it was selected. He had the gym bag with him. He looked around to see if anyone or anything looked at all familiar. Seeing nothing, he crossed to the northeast corner and checked his watch.

Less than a minute passed. A tall black kid in a New York Giants football jersey approached John.

"Is that the package?" the kid said.

"Yes. You have something for me?"

He took the bag from John. "Stay here," he said. "I'll be right back."

The kid in the number fifty-six jersey walked around the corner onto Quentin Road. Less than a minute later he returned with a message. This time, he looked John in the eye.

"The man is very, very angry," he said.

"That's too bad. Where is—"

"That bag didn't have what he was expecting."

"And he wasn't going to give me what I was expecting either, because he doesn't have it."

The kid started to say something, but the bishop cut him off.

"All right, now you listen to me. You tell him this.

Every word. You tell him I know who he is. You tell him I've known him since the day he was born. Tell him that I changed his wet and dirty diapers. You tell him that. Tell him if he doesn't stop this nonsense, I'll make sure he goes to prison for the rest of his God . . . forsaken life."

The bishop stepped into the street and hailed a taxi.

The kid walked back around the corner and delivered the bishop's message. Junior listened. He gave the kid the fifty dollars he'd promised, but he was distracted by something he saw through the window of a sandwich shop across the street.

Father James conducted the 11:00 a.m. Mass for the intention of Angelo Telentino's soul as requested by his son, Angelo Jr. For the second time that week, the sanctuary was filled, but there was no coffin in front of the altar. The body wouldn't be released until the medical examiner finished with it.

Junior sat in the front row with other members of his late father's organization, including Joey Sitriani and his two bodyguards. Junior brought some muscle of his own. Junior and Joey had a sit-down scheduled for later that day, in Joey's words, "to go over a few things," in the back room at a small Italian restaurant on 4th Avenue in Bay Ridge.

Barbara and Bobby were in a pew a few rows behind Junior. Josh was once again standing off to the side near the rear of the nave. The bishop wasn't in attendance.

After Mass, Father James expressed his personal condolences to Junior. "You know, Angelo," he said, "in light of all that's happened, this would be a good time for you to consider your own future."

"I'm doing a whole lot of considering, Father," Junior said, but he was more interested in some activity at the back of the church. Barbara and Bobby were talking to Josh. "Father, do you know who that guy is, talking to Barbara Quattrone?" Junior asked.

"Oh, yes, Angelo, I do. He's a reporter from St. Louis, where Father Michael attended seminary," he said. "He's a very nice young man."

Joey Sitriani stepped between Junior and Father James and handed a thick envelope to the priest. The new head of the Telentino-Calabrese family stood tall and rail-thin, wearing a black pinstriped suit, white open-collar shirt, and shined black French-toed shoes.

"Father, please accept this offering to St. Brendan's in memory of my close friend Angelo Telentino, *Senior*," he said. Then, turning to Junior, "I'll see you later, right, Angelo?"

"Right, Joey," Junior said. "I got some things to take care of first, but I'll see you at three o'clock."

"You behave yourself, Angelo," Joey said, pointing a finger at him. He and his posse walked toward the back of the church.

"Barbara," he said to her as he passed.

"Hello, Joey," she said.

He nodded his head a couple of times. "We should talk sometime soon, Barbara."

She didn't respond. Joey and his crew left the church.

"Great, just fucking great," she said, and quickly genuflected for cursing inside the church.

"Who's that?" Josh asked.

"I can't get away from these . . . people," she said. "Can we go somewhere? Get some coffee, maybe? Please?"

"Come on, Barbara," Bobby said. "Let's get out of here before—"

"Hey, Barbara," Junior shouted. "Don't you go anywhere!"

"Call my secretary," she said back to him. "Make an appointment." She, Bobby, and Josh walked to Josh's car. Mikey jumped into Dominic's car since Barbara and Bobby were together. They followed the trio at a distance.

Barbara directed Josh toward the Olympia Diner on Nostrand Avenue. "I can't tell who all these players are without a scorecard," Josh said. "They should be wearing uniforms with numbers on them."

"Orange jumpsuits is what they should be wearing," Barbara said. She told Josh that Joey Sitriani would be taking Angelo Telentino's place at the head of the family table.

"And the one who told you not to leave?" Joshua asked.

"Barbara . . ." Bobby said.

"That's Angelo's son, Angelo Jr.," she said. "We've known each other since we were kids. Things got complicated when . . . when our fathers had a falling out, you might say."

"Barbara, you just met this guy," Bobby said.

"You know," Josh said, "Bobby's right. You don't have to tell me anything you don't want to."

"I know," she said. "Turn right at the next light. Let me tell you what I—what we're up against here."

About fifteen minutes later they arrived at the Olympia. Josh couldn't believe the size of the menu. Bobby got a grilled cheese with fries, and Barbara ordered a Monte Cristo with a side of fresh fruit. Josh chose a western omelet, hash browns, and coffee.

Outside, Dominic punched a number into his mobile phone.

"Yeah, Dominic," Junior answered.

Dominic told him where they were. "They're here with some guy," Dominic said. "I don't know him, but he looks familiar."

Junior had a good idea who Barbara and Bobby were with. "All right," he said. "You and Mikey can take off. I got it from here."

"There aren't places in St. Louis other than IHOP or Denny's, maybe, to get breakfast like this in the middle of the afternoon," Josh said. They sat at a booth and waited for their food to be delivered.

"I was eighteen and Junior was fourteen when my father was killed by one of Angelo's people," Barbara said. "I don't know who pulled the trigger, but I always believed that the order came down from the top. Angelo swore to my mother and me that he found out who did it and got rid of him.

"Our mothers were like third cousins related through marriage," she said. "They died in a bad car accident coming home from Atlantic City. It was about two years after my father. Bobby's been with me since then."

"So, you and Angelo?" Joshua asked. Barbara looked at him, eyes flashing.

"Which one?" she asked.

"The father," Joshua said.

She told him how Angelo had been both looking out for and exploiting her ever since her mother died.

"He set me and Bobby up in an apartment and created a job for me in his organization as a courier." She took in a deep breath and looked into Josh's eyes.

"Don't go anywhere you don't want to go, Barbara," he said.

"I guess I was about twenty-two when Angelo paid me $5,000 . . . I'm not sure I want to tell you this."

"Why not?" Joshua asked.

"Because I like you and I want you to like me," she said.

"I already like you, Barbara," he said, smiling. "I don't judge people. I guess it's a byproduct of my work. We've all done things we're not especially proud of. What you tell me stays with me, and I promise it won't diminish you in my eyes."

"I don't need to hear this," Bobby said. "Old news." He took two quick bites of his sandwich and went outside.

"Junior was a virgin and Angelo wanted him to . . . have his first experience with a real woman."

Joshua managed to hide his anger. "He prostituted you?"

She looked away. "I didn't see it that way at the time," she said. "It was no big deal. I was experienced, and $5,000 all at one time was a ton of money for us."

"Okay," Josh said, exhaling. He nodded, encouraging her to go on.

"That wasn't the problem," she said. "The problem was, and is, because of a one- time thing, Junior thinks he loves me and has convinced himself that I love him."

"Even after all this time?"

"Yeah," she said. "Nothing else ever happened between us, but Angelo now had another way of using me, and every now and then he took advantage."

She'd spoken very matter-of-factly, but then she leaned in and looked at him with a previously unseen intensity. "I'm not unhappy that asshole is dead, but I'm really nervous about what it means, you know, with Junior."

"You don't believe Junior is going to try to take over the family, do you?"

"He may be thinking about it," she said, "but that guy, Joey Sitriani, the one we saw after the service? He'll put a stop to that in a hurry."

They worked on their food and maintained an uneasy silence. Then Barbara opened her eyes wide. "Oh, shit." She exhaled.

"What's wrong?"

"Mr. T., he was killed when?"

Josh went for his notebook. "Wednesday night or early Thursday morning, why?"

"I think—no, I'm pretty sure I know what happened to Mr. T."

# CHAPTER 9

Junior was not having a good day. First, he failed to close the deal with his uncle, and now some asshole was getting way to close to the only girl—woman—he'd ever loved. He watched Bobby from across Nostrand Avenue. He needed to get the jewels and see if he could move them through a fence he knew.

Barbara and Josh left the diner and were close to Josh's car when Junior pulled his CTS to a screeching stop. He blocked them from leaving and got out of his car.

"What the fuck is going on here, Barbara?" he said.

"Nothing that's any of your business, Angelo," she said. "I'm sorry about your father."

"I'll bet you're fucking sorry," he said. He turned toward Josh. "Who the fuck are you, and what are you doing with—"

"Junior, er, Angelo," Bobby said.

"I'll deal with you in a minute, you little prick," Junior said, pointing a finger at him. "You got something—"

"Look, Angelo, why don't you turn down the volume just a little," Josh said.

"I'll turn down your fucking volume, asshole." His face was inches from Joshua's. "I see you got a new car."

"Oh, that was you. Why am I not surprised?" Then, much more seriously, "You need to step back, Angelo, and you need to do it right now."

Instead, Junior reached behind him and retrieved a silver-plated H&K .357 he'd been carrying since his father's murder. In less time than it might take to sneeze, Josh relieved Junior of the weapon, landed a disorienting punch just over the bridge of his nose, then grabbed Junior's arm and twisted it behind his back. He whispered into Junior's ear.

"I can break your arm right now, or you can step away, get in your car, and think about what you're doing. What are you going to do?"

"I'm gonna fucking kill you, I'm gonna kill your family, I'm gonna kill these two—" Joshua tightened his grip and turned Junior's arm.

"Yeah," Josh said. "But you're going to do all that with your left hand unless I break that one also."

"Okay, okay, okay," Junior said. Joshua let go, unlocked the car doors and told Barbara and Bobby to get inside. He released the magazine from the handgun, pulled the slide to eject the round from the chamber, handed the empty gun back to Junior, and took two steps back. He watched as Junior worked his shoulder then got into his CTS and put the window down.

"This isn't over, asshole," he said, driving off. Josh watched him peel out of the parking lot and onto Nostrand Avenue.

"Where'd you learn how to do that stuff?" Bobby asked.

Josh guided the car back in the general direction of St. Brendan's. "It's nothing," Josh said. "You could learn it."

"That could have been ugly," Barbara said.

"You know," Joshua said, "based on what you just told me about Mr. T, I think it's time we had a conversation with the bishop." Josh called the bishop, who agreed to meet them at a church near his office.

"Barbara," Bobby said, "maybe we should tell him, you know?"

Barbara turned in her seat and looked hard at Bobby. She took a deep breath. "Okay, little brother," she said. "You tell Josh what that asshole made you do."

Bobby laid out everything that happened when Junior and he robbed Father Michael. Josh didn't ask any questions, but when Bobby was done, Josh turned to Barbara.

"Tell me again about this DeSantis guy."

She recounted her two conversations with Mr. T, and then her play with Billy DeSantis. "The good news is nothing happened, but the timing, based on what

Mr. T told me, means Billy easily could have been the last person to see Angelo and Carmine alive."

Everyone was quiet for a few minutes. Barbara gave Josh directions on how to get to the Holy Name of Jesus Church on Prospect Park West.

"How do you know how to get everywhere in this city?" Josh asked her. "St. Louis is a big city, but you could put about eight of them into this place."

She laughed. "I go to and from places all over the city every day," she said. "It's my job to know how to get around."

"Billy DeSantis never told you directly what his business was with Mr. T, right?" Josh asked.

"No, but I got his business card while he was napping," she said. She fished it out of her purse. "Here it is, DeSantis Management. Ft. Lauderdale, Florida," she said. "I wonder what he did for Mr. T."

Josh pulled into a spot across the street from the church. The three of them walked in.

Bobby and Barbara dipped a finger into a small silver bowl containing holy water inside the entrance. The bishop was seated in a pew in the middle of the church. After they genuflected, the three of them sat down in the row behind the bishop. John turned and faced the three of them.

"First of all, Joshua," he said, "I'm concerned that you're losing objectivity and getting way too personally involved in things here."

Josh had been aware of the potential for this since

he arrived in Brooklyn. "How can I not, sir? This all started when my brother, who I never got to know, was murdered during the commission of a robbery."

"Oh, man," Bobby said. "That's why you look so much like him." He started sobbing. "I'm sorry, I am so sorry . . ."

"Of course," the bishop said, ignoring Bobby. "But these are very dangerous people, and I don't want to see anything happen to you. To any of you."

"Yeah, I'm pretty sure he can handle himself," Barbara said. She recounted the episode in the parking lot at the diner.

"Let's see what we know, what we think we know, and what we need to do," Josh said, "because, at some point, we're going to need to get the police involved."

John started to speak but hesitated.

"What is it, Your Excellency?" Barbara said.

He let out a sigh. "Barbara, I'm trying to protect your brother if I possibly can," he said. "I don't think he's to blame for what happened. Bobby was Junior's pawn. I have an idea, but I need to do some additional research before sharing it."

Barbara told the bishop an abbreviated version of her conversation with Mr. T and her subsequent encounter with Billy DeSantis.

"He came to see me the same day my brother was murdered," the bishop said. "He brought me money from a personal account he manages for me. I was going to use it to buy back the jewels, but, after your visit the other day, I decided I'd let him know I knew what had happened instead of letting him have the easy payday he'd imagined."

The bishop got out of his pew and led them behind the altar, toward the door that led to the sacristy. "You know, my brother had an account with Billy DeSantis as well."

"So, you think he was bringing money to Angelo also?" Josh asked. Barbara nodded agreement.

"It makes sense," he said. "Angelo told me the day before that he'd handle it, but I didn't want anything from him."

Barbara nodded. "Mr. T told me Billy DeSantis was bringing an important package. That much money is definitely an important package." John began to speak, but Barbara wasn't finished. "It all fits," she said. "Angelo tells me to entertain Billy. The next day he brings money to you, and then he has dinner with Angelo. Later that night, Angelo and his driver end up murdered."

"What do we do now?" Josh asked.

"At some point, I'm going to have to sit down with Lieutenant Otis," John said. "I believe I can lead him in the right direction on the robbery and Father Michael's death." Josh asked John to hold off on that meeting while he and Barbara kicked some things around.

"Let me get with you tomorrow on that, sir," Josh said.

"Will I go to jail?" Bobby asked. "I deserve to go to jail."

"Nobody's going to jail just yet," John said. "How do we get Mr. DeSantis back to New York?"

"I can make that happen," Barbara said. "He's a sleaze. He'll take my call."

Both the bishop and Josh objected strenuously. She smiled and shook her head. "Yeah, yeah, I know," she said. "I'm just a girl. Let me remind you both, I've been on my own for a long time," she said. "And I've been dealing with these scumbags, pardon me, Bishop, for all of that time. I can handle men when I need to."

Josh and John looked at each other and shrugged.

"I can do this," she said. "We can do this."

Junior's meeting with Joey Sitriani worked out okay in that he was still breathing air instead of standing in concrete somewhere in Lower New York Bay. Surrounded by most of the major players in the Telentino-Calabrese family, Joey let Junior know who was in charge. "There's a structure in place for a reason, Angelo," Joey told him. "Don't make the mistake of thinking because he was your father that you inherit his business. This is not that kind of business. Now, let me lay out how things are gonna work moving forward."

Joey took nearly three hours describing the organization's structure and how it would operate under his leadership. He talked about the other families in the city and how they were going to do business with them. Joey told everyone present his job, territory, and responsibilities from that moment forward.

"Out of respect for your father," he said to Junior, "you'll have an important role and the same opportunity for future leadership as anyone else in the room. Do your job. Be a good soldier. You'll be fine."

Junior had other issues to deal with and didn't need the problem of a turf war. He decided he'd do what was in his own best interest. "I'm in, Joey. Thank you for the opportunity." There were hugs and kisses all around.

Angelo was seated in the office inside his father's apartment considering his next steps. The facts were, he didn't get the money, and he didn't have the jewels. The latter, he might be able to fix. The former, he had no idea what to do about.

He found the key to a locked desk drawer, opened it, and began leafing through files. There were real estate holdings, automobile registrations, and insurance policies, all in his father's name. He came upon a hanging folder with the handwritten label, "DeSantis." In the file he found account statements indicating his father had just over $13 million invested with De-Santis Management in something called REITs. He plowed through everything still on the desk but found nothing to indicate the account had ever been closed.

"Fuck," he whispered. "Fuck, fuck, fuck!" he shouted. He dialed Billy DeSantis's phone number.

"This is Billy."

"This is Angelo Telentino, you prick. I'm looking at a statement from DeSantis Management dated three months ago showing a balance of a little over $13 million in a bunch of REITs. *Three months ago!* So, tell me again your bullshit story about how my father closed his account with you eight months ago."

"I don't know what you're looking at, Angelo, but the Angelo Telentino who did business with me, and who is now hopefully enjoying the company of the angels and saints, closed his account last year and took all the proceeds *in cash*. I advised against it, but he knew what he wanted to do. Now, I know this because I delivered the cash to him myself, probably to the same apartment in Brooklyn you're screaming at me from."

Junior took in a deep breath to control his rage. "You're not playing with the kids on the corner, asshole," he said. "I'm going to pay you a visit down there in Florida. And if you don't come up with what's mine, I'm going to carve you up like a fucking Christmas ham. You want to avoid that, you got three days to *get me my fucking money!*" He slammed down the phone.

# CHAPTER 10

"Really?" Barbara asked. "You cook?"

"Hey, I'm a Renaissance guy, Barbara," Josh said. "I pick out and buy my own clothes. I listen to NPR on the radio, watch Discovery on TV. I even read books, and yes, on occasion, I cook."

Josh, Barbara, and Bobby were in Barbara's living room. After dinner, they would drive to Queens to drop Bobby off for a couple of days with an uncle and aunt on their mother's side. With what they had planned, they didn't need to be distracted by anything Junior might try with Bobby. Josh told them he'd take care of dinner.

"What's on the menu?" Bobby asked, warming to the new guy in his sister's life.

"Well," Josh said, "I'm certainly not going to even attempt Italian food. I'm thinking steaks, baked potatoes, seasoned vegetables . . . you know, like that."

"Sounds pretty good, Mr. Abrahams," said Barbara. They all looked at one another when they heard a knock at the door. Josh smiled. "I got this." He walked down the hallway, looked through the peephole, and opened the door.

"St. Louis?" the delivery service driver asked.

"That's me," Josh said, handing the driver four twenties. "Are we all good here?"

"We are awesome!" the driver said and handed Josh the shopping bag. "Thanks a bunch."

He walked back to living room. "Dinner, compliments of Outback Steakhouse," he said.

"I thought you were cooking," Bobby said.

"I said I'd take care of dinner, young fella," Josh said. "You have to pay attention."

Barbara took the bag into the dining area outside the kitchen, set the table, offered thanks, and they sat down for a good meal.

They drove Bobby to Maspeth to stay with his aunt and uncle. Bobby was under strict lockdown for the next two or three days, depending on how quickly the plan they had designed played out.

"I'm way off the reservation here," Josh told Barbara after they came back to her apartment. "I came here to write a story, which is what I do, but this has turned into so much more. I hope I still have a job when I get home."

"What are you talking about?" Barbara asked.

"Reporters need be detached from the things they

report," he said. "Once we put this plan in motion, I'll be doing a lot more than just observing and reporting."

"That assumes the cops even let us go down this road," she said.

"Here's the thing. The brother I never knew is dead. I just had dinner with someone directly involved in the crime I came to investigate. Now I'm alone with this great-looking woman who is the sister of the guy involved. And never mind all the Telentino family connections. This particular slope is the definition of slippery."

Barbara came and sat on Josh's lap, put her arms around his neck, and kissed him long and hard. He returned the favor.

"I don't know anything about any of that," she said. "I just know that you are the first decent guy I've met in a hell of a long time, and even though it's only been a few days, I am not gonna let you get away without a fight."

Josh considered the train that was about to leave the station. He knew he was opening a potentially dark, dangerous door. He really liked this woman, this Barbara Quattrone, but she was somehow involved up to her lovely neck in the very story he was chasing. He pushed his trepidation out of the way in the face of the urgency he was feeling. He'd have to worry about ethics and professional propriety some other time.

They tumbled onto her bed, wrestling with each other's clothing, all the while kissing and feeling and attempting not to end up on the floor. Josh was almost a head taller than she was, but he was attracted to shorter, more compact women. It became clear that both of them had been experiencing something of a dry spell because, before they knew it, they'd finished before either of them really wanted it to end.

The rest of the night was a blur of disjointed conversation about their lives, their goals, their histories, their thoughts about the future, and the events that had brought them together. There was also a whole lot more of getting to know each other's bodies. Before they slipped, for however short a period of time, into blessed rest, Josh knew he liked Barbara a lot. And she seemed to like him.

At some point in the middle of the night Josh resolved that, if he couldn't manage to write the story objectively, he'd take a sabbatical from the paper and turn the whole affair into a book. He also allowed himself to wonder if there was a place in his life for Barbara back home in St. Louis. It was way too early to bring her in on any of that. So much could go wrong if you assumed you knew how people were going to react in dangerous, stressful situations.

For now, Josh's goals were to get Junior to own the robbery and killing of Father Michael, and to get Billy DeSantis to incriminate himself in the murders of Angelo Telentino and Carmine Calabrese. Josh knew how to push buttons in an interview setting. Barbara knew how to handle men. Maybe between the two of them, they could pull this off. After breakfast they decided that they, not Bishop Telentino, would bring Det. Lt. Quinn Otis up to date on what they were thinking. As far as the bishop was concerned, for now, the less he knew the better. Before they went any further, Barbara and Josh brought the beige drawstring sack containing the Telentino family's jewels to Father James at St. Brendan's. They needed to be somewhere unconnected to her and her brother until this was all over.

After they returned from St. Brendan's, Barbara retrieved Billy DeSantis's business card and dialed his number.

"This is Billy," he said.

"Hey Billy, this is Betsy," she said. "We met at the Sherry-Netherland last week. Remember?"

He sucked in a deep breath. "Yeah, I remember," he said. "How could I forget you? How'd you get my number?"

She laughed. "You don't remember giving me your business card?" she asked. "I know you had other things on your mind, and I know we had a lot of wine, but—"

"Yeah, yeah, I remember, I remember," he lied. "So how are you doing, Betsy? Where are you?"

"So, here's what I'm thinking, Billy," she said. "And please, pay close attention, okay?"

Billy started to reply but she rolled right over him. "The night after you and I, well, you remember. The next night, I'm guessing you and Angelo Telentino had dinner. Probably, if I know him, and I do, or I did, you ate at the Luna down on Mulberry Street. How am I doing so far?"

Billy didn't say anything.

"Okay, let's just assume I'm doing fine. You know, Angelo told me that you were coming into town and that you were bringing him a *very important* package. His words: 'Very important.' I'm going to take a shot here and say that very important package was maybe about, oh, $250,000 in cash. You don't have to answer. I know I'm right. He also told me to show you a really good time but to not let you think it was a set up." Barbara sat down. "Sorry, Billy. It was. A set up."

"You work for Angelo Telentino?" he asked.

"Past tense," she said. "Obviously. You know, him being dead and all that. And just so you know, that good time you thought you had? It didn't happen. Here's the thing, Billy. Right now, I'm the only person, the only person still alive, anyway, maybe besides a little old lady in Little Italy and a hotel desk clerk and a waiter at the Sherry, who knows for sure you were in town to see Angelo Telentino. And I know, based on what reporters are saying, he and his nephew were found dead right after you and he had cannoli. And I'm thinking that just maybe you had something to do with this . . . unfortunate and untimely event. Now, I'm sure you cleaned all your prints out of his SUV, but maybe not. I'm sure your handsome face is on security video in at least a few places, and who knows what interest the police might have in this kind of information. Are you following me, Billy?"

"What are we talking about here, Betsy?" he asked. "I know we had a good time together. You left me a note, and you left me some—a souvenir, right? So, what is this, some kind of shakedown?"

She smiled at Josh, put a finger into her mouth, and pulled at her cheek, mimicking a hook in a fish's mouth.

"Such an ugly word, Billy," she said. "We're talking about a hundred thousand dollars, cash, delivered to me, same hotel, tomorrow night. No nonsense, no games, no bullshit, no excuses. If you hurry, you can catch the Amtrak and get into the city by late tomorrow afternoon. You told me you don't fly, remember? You can even use the room after we conclude our business."

"Are you out of your fucking mind? Who the fuck do you think you are? Do you know who you're fucking dealing with here? I can turn you into ground beef by tomorrow night. I can—"

"Here's what you can do, asshole," she said. "You make sure you're knocking at my door at the Sherry tomorrow night at 8:00 p.m. Not before, not after. You make sure you're alone and that you bring the money in cash. And know that I'll do exactly what I told you I'll do if you're even five minutes late. Now you have a nice rest of your day, Mr. Billy DeSantis Management."

She hung up the burner phone Josh had bought an hour earlier at a nearby Duane Reade, let out a big breath, and started laughing.

Josh looked at her in wonder. "You are, without question, totally and completely, the most badass woman I have ever met," he said. "I can't believe you. I would give anything to be a fly on the wall wherever he is right now."

Next, Barbara called Junior. She told Josh she felt not a single shred of remorse about how she would deal with him. He was responsible for the death of a well-liked young priest, the brother of a guy she now cared about a lot. He'd stolen something important to his own uncle and to his late grandmother. He'd jammed her brother up, and he thought he had some messed-up claim on her from something that had happened years earlier. And his father was an asshole.

"Listen, Angelo, you and I need to talk," she began.

"You're goddam right we need to talk, Barbara," he said. "Your kid brother has something of mine, and I need to get it from him today."

"Yeah," she said, "that's not gonna happen, Junior. I'm not in the city today and won't be back until late tomorrow afternoon."

"You out with that scumbag you were with yesterday?" he asked. "That guy is already dead. He just doesn't know it."

She looked at the phone and shook her head. "Oh, Angelo," she said, almost kindly, "you really don't have a clue, do you? Bobby told me everything the day after it happened. Those jewels you were counting on? They're already back where they belong. You're all by yourself, Angelo, and you're on the hook for Father Mike. That ship is going to sail sometime real soon. But that's not why we need to talk."

There was a long pause, then Junior spoke. "Barbara, you can't. Your brother will go to jail. When can we talk?" She heard the desperation.

"Junior, just listen," she said. "I know who killed your father. I'm not a hundred percent sure why, but I'm guessing it had to do with money, a lot of money. These things usually do. Just plan to meet me tomorrow at 6:00 p.m. at the Sherry-Netherland. You know where that is?"

"Yeah," he said. "My father used to take meetings there."

"I'll text you the room number," she said. "The guy? He's going to be in town tomorrow. I'll talk to you then." She hung up, exhaled again, and looked at Josh.

"Okay," Josh said. "My turn." He dialed the number for the 71st precinct. "Detective Lieutenant Quinn Otis, please," he said. "My name is Josh Abrahams. Please tell him it's important."

# CHAPTER 11

Bishop Telentino wore street clothes for the ride into Manhattan on the M train. He got off near 6th Avenue and W. 47th Street. He carried a small messenger bag containing a square box holding the jewels his mother had left in his care. He'd collected them from Father Jimmy earlier that morning.

A particular gem dealer in New York's diamond district specialized in stones with historical significance. Unlike most other dealers on W. Forty-Seventh, Belgians operated Jacobus Jewels, not Hassidic Jews or Israelis.

In a small space on the sixth floor of the same building that housed the Gemological Institute of America, about a dozen times a week a handful of highly skilled gemologists and historians evaluated stones either believed or known to be of historical importance and, in rare cases, extraordinary value.

The bishop pressed a button at the door marked

simply "Jacobus." A voice asked for his name. "John Telentino," he said. He was buzzed inside.

A very large man of indeterminate heritage and with nothing resembling a neck occupied virtually the entire area of a small anteroom. He turned and punched numbers into a keypad on the wall, which unlocked another door.

"Good day, Bishop," a small professorial-looking man said. He had the hint of a European accent, wispy brown hair, and bright blue eyes. He wore thick rimless glasses. He stood before a table filled with magnifying glasses, things that resembled dental tools, about a dozen large old books, and a clipboard with a single sheet of paper. "My name is Joseph Lambert. I'm one of the principals here at Jacobus. I'm anxious to see what you have."

"I'm not exactly sure what I have, Mr. Lambert," John said. "I am hoping you can enlighten me." He provided the information his mother had given him about the age and family provenance of the jewels. He also explained he had absolutely nothing in the way of what might constitute legal proof of ownership. "She told me they've been in our family for over twenty generations," he said. "That would put them at, what, at least five hundred years old?"

"Let's have a look, okay?"

John unfastened the bag; took out the box; and, from inside the beige velvet pouch, lifted two strings of blue, red, and green stones, some large and seemingly uncut, others smaller and expertly faceted. The jewels were connected to one another by thick dark brown wire. There were larger stones separated by pearls and smaller precious gems of various sizes and shapes. The strings, laid end to end, measured just short of 120 inches in length. "Hmmm," Lambert said. "Nearly three meters."

After a few moments of superficial inspection, followed by stone-by-stone examination with a jeweler's loupe, Joseph Lambert sat down, replaced his eyeglasses, crossed his hands in his lap, and looked at John.

"What did you tell me is your family name? Or, I suppose more importantly, your mother's family name?"

"Our family name is Telentino. My mother's family name was Conti."

"Do you know much about your family lineage and history?"

"I believe my mother's father may have landed at Ellis Island," John said. "He would have been a Conti. I don't know my grandmother's maiden name, and I don't know much at all about the Telentino side of the family. All things considered, I believe, at least on his side, they originated in Sicily."

While John sat patiently, Lambert leafed through a couple of his books. John caught glimpses of pictures but few with any clarity. When the gemologist finally found what he was looking for, he marked the page with a strip of cloth and closed the book. He took off his glasses and rubbed his eyes.

"Please, sir, sit down," he said. "I hope you have a few minutes. We have much to discuss."

Quinn Otis had commandeered three adjoining rooms at the Sherry-Netherland Hotel on the NYPD's American Express Gold Card. The NYPD's technical response services unit equipped the middle room with elaborate sound and picture capture. Neither Barbara nor Josh would be inhibited by having to wear electronic devices. Otis set up a command post in one of the adjoining rooms and left the third room for a small team of elite tactical services officers in the event that things didn't go according to plan. Now, back at the 71st Precinct, he was thinking of calling it all off.

"For the umpteenth time, I hate citizens doing these things," Otis said.

"And, once again, Detective, doing it this way helps us avoid the strong potentiality of one or both of these clowns lawyering up," Josh said.

At first Otis resisted, but the interrelationships and specifics were extremely compelling. With a whole lot of planning and a little bit of luck, he should be able to gift wrap a couple of extremely high-profile cases for his command structure, the New York and Kings

County district attorneys, and the voracious horde of New York media.

"I want to get every word of this on record," he said, "to cover my own ass in case something, anything, goes sideways, you know?"

Josh and Barbara walked Otis and his partner through every step of their plan. The partner was Marge Rucker, a serious, hard-boiled black female detective, who'd been working major crimes for fifteen years. She'd been the lead detective on some of Brooklyn's highest-profile arrests.

When they finished, Barbara said, "By about 9:30 tonight, you'll have two killers in custody and all it's going to cost you is a pass for my brother. Are we good?"

Marge Rucker nodded. "If how you laid it out works, we can discuss your brother," she said.

"Okay, then. We're done here," Josh said. "See you all later."

Barbara paced back and forth in front of the closed bathroom door in her apartment. "Come on, dude," she said, "you're worse than a woman. What are you doing in there?"

"Making my father happy," Josh said.

"Can't you make him happy later?" she asked, "Or maybe tomorrow?"

"Just a few more minutes," Josh said. "I'm finishing up."

"We need to be at the Sherry by six," she said. She heard the water running and then a toilet flushing. "You need to flush first, then you wash your hands"— the door opened—"Holy Mary, Mother of God."

"No," Josh said. "Just me." Josh had shaved his beard and mustache off and combed his hair to match the picture at Father Michael's funeral.

"That is very, um . . . wow!" Barbara said.

Josh shrugged. "Twins," he said. "Bound to be a strong resemblance, no?"

She took his face in her hands and kissed him full on the lips. "Okay," she said, disengaging. "That's wrong. I feel like I just kissed a dead priest." Josh laughed and hugged her.

"Let's just hope Junior has the same experience, but without the whole, you know, kissing thing," Josh said. He was wearing a black shirt, black Dockers, and black shoes—everything priestly black except the collar.

"I'm glad my brother isn't here," she said. "He'd never recover. Come on. Let's get into the city."

"Okay, I need to ask you something," Josh said. "Why do New Yorkers call Manhattan 'the city'?"

"Have you ever been there?" she asked him.

"Actually, no, I haven't been there yet," he said. "But isn't Brooklyn in the city? And Queens?"

"Technically, yes," she said. "And the Bronx and Staten Island. There are five boroughs in New York

City. But when you live in the outer boroughs, the four that aren't Manhattan, then Manhattan is"—she made air quotes—"'the city.'"

"I don't understand," he said.

"You will."

Barbara drove Josh's rental car against normal rush hour traffic. They swung from the Belt Parkway onto the Gowanus Expressway and, minutes later, onto the BQE. Josh took in the sheer immensity of New York City when Barbara made the sweeping turn that often provides the first glimpse a visitor gets of the lower Manhattan skyline. It was a gorgeous spring day, late April, late afternoon.

"Oh, man," he said, seeing the financial district, the Brooklyn Bridge, and towering over it all, Freedom Tower, the new building near the site of the World Trade Center's twin towers. "I get it now," he said. "*The* city, right?"

"Welcome to New York, country boy," she said, smiling.

"Country boy? We've got over 2.5 million people in metro St. Louis."

She laughed at him. "Dude, 2.5 million people live in Brooklyn. Some people call Brooklyn the borough of churches and trees. This," she waved her hand at the skyline and then toward uptown Manhattan as she eased onto the ramp for the Brooklyn Bridge, "*this* is what New Yorkers call, the city."

She took the FDR Drive uptown. On the way,

they talked themselves through the logistics of their meeting with Junior. The job was to get him to cop to the robbery and accidental killing of Michael while ignoring, or at least minimizing, Bobby's role. Barbara was certain she could handle Junior, especially once he got a glimpse of what he would view as the face of the man he believed he'd killed.

The second meeting, with Billy DeSantis, would be more complicated. First of all, he had planned and executed the killing of a major organized crime figure and his bodyguard. He'd gotten away without a trace, almost. Mama Luna had called the police as soon as she heard the news of Mr. T's murder. She gave detectives a very good description of the man he'd brought with him to dinner but couldn't remember his name, just that he was from Florida. The counter man at Ferrara's also gave a good description, so New York police had a picture of the last person to see Angelo Telentino alive.

The plan was for Barbara to lure him into the room. After he was inside and she was outside, Josh would take over and either squeeze out a confession or elicit enough to provide the cops in the adjoining room sufficient cause to hold DeSantis while they collected forensic evidence tying him to the murders.

Josh had been quiet for a while.

"Eight million dollars for your thoughts," Barbara said to him.

He smiled. "Only eight million?" He took a drink

from a bottle of spring water. "I'm just thinking about how stuff happens in such random ways. From the time I was a kid, I knew I was adopted and I knew I had a brother, but I didn't know anything about him. I didn't know anything about my birth parents. Still don't. If Michael didn't walk to the bank, get mugged, and then die, I'd still be reporting and writing news in St. Louis. I wouldn't know Bishop Telentino, you . . ."

She looked at him. "I'm really sorry about Father Mike. Everybody loved him, but I'm really glad to know you, Joshua Abrahams. And I think he'd have been glad to know you too."

Josh smiled at her and put his hand on her leg. "So," he said, "you and Billy DeSantis, nothing happened? Really?"

She laughed. "He thinks something happened," she said, "but he didn't even get to first base. Asshole had a serious good night's sleep, though."

In his office, Bishop John Telentino dialed a number with a 314-area code.

"Henry Abrahams," a voice said at the other end.

"Mr. Abrahams, my name is John Telentino. I've recently made the acquaintance of your son, Joshua."

"Josh has mentioned you quite often in the past week or so. We talk almost every day. I'm terribly sorry for your loss—your losses.

John took a sip from his water glass. "Thank you,

Mr. Abrahams. Your son is a splendid young man. I hope you and Mrs. Abrahams are justifiably proud of the wonderful job you did raising him."

"We are, sir. And thank you. Now, how may I be of assistance?"

"This is very difficult for me to ask. Considering recent developments here, some of which I imagine you know or have heard about, I'm asking your permission to share some . . . personal history matters with your son." There was a moment of silence at the other end of the line.

"I think I know what you're asking, Bishop."

"And you're an attorney, so I know you know I have to ask permission."

"I can't consent to that without consulting his mother, Bishop," Henry Abrahams said. "Might I return your call in about an hour?"

"Of course, Mr. Abrahams. And please, call me John."

"I will, but only if you'll call me Henry."

# CHAPTER 12

Barbara pulled into a garage on E. 62nd Street just east of 5th Avenue. It left a three-block walk to the Sherry. She pulled a small wheeled overnight bag holding changes of clothes, cosmetics, and two small personal recording devices Josh wanted in order to document whatever happened for his own purposes. There was no need for her and Josh to check in. They took the elevator up to the eleventh floor and knocked on the door to Detective Lieutenant Otis's command center.

Inside, Josh and Barbara went over the plan to deal with Angelo. Otis and Rucker were on board but balked when Barbara demanded a total pass for Bobby. They were backed up by an assistant district attorney from Kings County, who was in the room.

"There are a bunch of reasons why your brother has to do at least minimal time," Rucker said. "He was part of a mugging and robbery where someone was killed, Ms. Quattrone, even though it was probably unintentional."

Barbara was ready to bolt. "We're going to give you two high-profile wins tonight," she said, nose to nose with Rucker. Otis and Josh just spectated this little tête-à-tête between two strong, willful women. "You need to figure something out that includes my brother walking on this. He's already given you enough to convict Angelo for Father Mike's death and the robbery."

Otis attempted to referee. "Have you spoken to Bishop Telentino yet today?"

"No," she said. "What does he have to do with this?"

"I guess that means he hasn't told you yet. He's arranged for Bobby to enter a seminary near St. Louis next year if he's able to complete four college prerequisites first," Otis said. "The soonest he can do that is next fall. Here's what we propose. Bobby does county time, in Brooklyn, until he's ready to leave and go to school. It gives the DA over there something to work with, and it gives Bobby a chance at an excellent future."

Barbara looked at Josh. He gave her a single small nod. She looked over at the Assistant District Attorney.

"This is a good deal for him, Barbara," the ADA said. "If we get done what we expect with Junior, there'll be no trial, no testifying, and, most important, no state time." And I can sweeten it. He cops to involuntarily aiding and abetting. The 'involuntary' means he didn't know about anything until he got into that car with Telentino. He agrees to six months of county time, gets out in three, and after a year with no criminal behavior, his record is wiped clean. His whole role in what happened vanishes. Ms. Quattrone, we don't want to jam him up, but he needs to take responsibility for some really bad judgment."

Reluctantly, Barbara agreed to the deal. She used the bathroom to freshen her makeup while Otis and Rucker told Josh his resemblance to Father Michael was scary.

Once Barbara emerged, she and Josh received a key card from Rucker and went into the room next door, looking to anyone who might see them like a young couple getting ready for a night on the town. It was 5:30 p.m., and Angelo was scheduled to arrive in half an hour.

Billy was angry. The entire Amtrak trip was an exercise in controlling his seething rage. *Who does this slut think she's playing with? Does she really believe she can shake down Billy DeSantis?*

In addition to the Telentino brothers, only one of whom was still filling his lungs, Billy worked for almost three dozen very bad people. He had laundered tens of millions of dollars in dirty money. Through his father's and, after Pete died, his own conservative investment program, his clients enjoyed upmarket returns and IRS-audit-proof asset protection. The mob never forgot the lessons learned from the experience involving Al Capone.

Billy planned to slowly and carefully liquidate the REITs Angelo Telentino's $13 million portfolio partially funded, starting in three weeks. The proceeds would be spread into accounts in a dozen small banks throughout western Europe. These banks were safe, chartered with powerful secrecy policies, and shielded by tight national laws. Plus, the funds were easily accessible without him having to fly anywhere.

Once he disposed of Betsy, the blackmailing bitch, he'd head home to Florida with no one still alive any the wiser.

Billy needed to calm down in order to execute his plan, just as he'd executed the plan less than a week earlier. He'd already arranged to pick up another package from Milos's Chinatown resource. He'd play by Betsy's rules only until he had her behind the closed door of her Sherry suite. The cash in his gym bag was flash money. It would be heading back to Ft. Lauderdale with him after he'd finished with her. Just to confuse things further, he had a reservation to spend the night in a downtown Philadelphia hotel.

He wished he had time to take in a private high-stakes poker game he knew of in the city or for a quick trip to Atlantic City, but that would have to wait. He needed to stick to his plan if he was to once and for all get away with the contents of Angelo Telentino's investment account.

At five minutes before six there was a spirited knock on the door of a room on the eleventh floor of the Sherry-Netherland hotel. Barbara let Junior in and locked the door.

"Sit in that chair," she said, pointing to the wingback near the window. A small recording device on the table holding the flat panel TV would see, hear, and record everything. Barbara pulled the upholstered chair from in front of the table, sat down, and crossed her legs.

"You look nice, Barbara," Junior said. She was wearing a simple black dress, low cut and hemmed about three inches above her knees.

"Thanks, but that's not why we're here, Angelo."

Josh stepped out from the bathroom and stood framed against the inside of the door to the room. Junior jumped to his feet and pointed at him.

"Who . . . what the fuck is this? You're dead. I was at your funeral. I . . ."

"You were at my brother's funeral, Angelo," Josh said. "My twin brother. You robbed him, you killed him, and now you're going to pay for what you did."

Junior lunged past Barbara, tackled Josh and the two went to the ground. Josh's RMA training kicked in; he immediately turned Junior over and pushed the heels of his palms into the soft spaces just below Junior's shoulders.

"Don't make me hurt you, Angelo," Josh said, emphasizing every word. "I really don't want to hurt you.

But if you don't get your shit together and settle down, I promise you'll lose the use of both your arms for six or seven weeks. Do you want that? Do you?"

Otis and Rucker watched as Barbara, staring into the camera, shook her head no, over and over again. Josh had assured them he could handle almost anything close up that happened, and he was doing just that.

Junior squirmed, trying to get out from under Josh's weight on his gut. The effect of Josh's thumbs pressing into Junior's shoulders was terribly painful. He relaxed and shook his head. "Let me up," he said. "I'm done."

Josh stood up an extended a hand to Junior. He pulled him up and patted him down. "Come on, Angelo," he said. "Let's do this."

Junior slumped into his chair. "Nobody was supposed to die," he said. "No one was even supposed to get hurt. It was an accident. I just . . . we just wanted those jewels." He swallowed hard. "I just wanted a score so I could . . ."

"So you could what, Angelo?" Barbara asked.

Angelo looked at her. He let his eyes roam around the room. He looked at Josh and shook his head. "I wanted my own money," he said. "I was always gonna be my father's son. That's it. Anything I wanted to do had to go through him. When I was fifty, I'd still only be Angelo Telentino Jr. I wanted to be someone, something else." Junior looked from one to the other. "So, what now?"

Josh sat down on the bed. "Now you cop to what you did and hope you can avoid life in prison."

"Ah, fuck, I know you," Junior said. "You're that goddam reporter." He looked at Barbara. "You threw me over for this guy? What about us, Barbara? What about us?"

Barbara moved her chair closer to Angelo's and took his hands in hers. "Junior, there is no us. There never was any *us*!"

"How can you say that? You and me, we have history. I love you, Barbara. I've always loved you, ever since . . ."

He was a study in physical and emotional pain. Barbara almost wished she didn't have to do what she knew she had to do.

"Angelo, your piece of shit father paid me to be with you," she said. "He set me and Bobby up in our apartment, he gave me a job, and he used me. He wanted me to be your first. I needed help after . . . after he had my father killed, and then our mothers died, so I did what he wanted me to do."

"He paid you to be with me? That wasn't real?"

"I'm not proud of it, Angelo, but I did what I had to do. I never loved you. We were friends. Childhood friends. Nothing more. I'm sorry, but it is what it is."

"I can't believe this. He paid you?"

"Focus, Angelo. Now you have to do what you can to survive. That means you come clean about the robbery and try to make a deal that doesn't include you never seeing daylight again."

She couldn't tell how much he heard of what she'd said to him. She could see the wheels turning in his head, and then he sprung out of his chair. Josh moved between Junior and her.

"You don't want to make things worse, Angelo," Josh said. "I'm not going to let you touch her, and if I have to, I promise I will really hurt you. You know I can do this, so do yourself a favor, sit back down and listen."

Josh signaled to Barbara that he'd handle it from here. She went into the bathroom while Josh directed Junior into a chair and sat down in front of him.

"Here's what's going to happen, Angelo," he said. "The police have been watching and listening to everything that's been said and done since you walked in here. They're in the next room. You're going to spend time in there with Lieutenant Otis, Detective Rucker, and a Kings County ADA. You need to figure out how to best help yourself."

Junior's eyes darted around the hotel room, then he lowered his head. "I got nothing to deal with," he said, staring at his shoes. "Nothing."

"Actually, Angelo, that may not be entirely accurate," Josh said. "You met with the new head of the family, right? Joey something?"

"Yeah, Joey Sitriani. It should have been me. It was my father's family. It's the Telentino-Calabrese family."

"You can't be your father's son only when it suits you, Angelo," Josh said.

Barbara came out of the bathroom and sat down on the bed. Angelo couldn't take his eyes off her.

"Angelo," Josh said. "Look at me. You met with him on Sunday, right?"

"Yeah, he laid out the new organization. So what?"

"You need to think about yourself, Angelo. Meet with the people next door and make yourself valuable to them. Who knows? Maybe they can help you with the Assistant DA," Josh said. "The DA's office deals all the time when they can reel in a much bigger fish."

"I guess I know a lot," Junior said. The door between the two rooms opened. Otis and Rucker walked in.

"Angelo Telentino Jr.," Otis said, "you're under arrest for the robbery and felony murder of Father Michael Olivetti. Please stand up."

Rucker put handcuffs on him and steered Angelo toward the room next door. Barbara wasn't enjoying this. She could have been a good friend if Angelo were able to think of her in that way.

"Detective," Josh said. "I need a few minutes with your prisoner before you start your interrogation. We still have another fish to catch."

Junior looked at Barbara. "You said you know who killed my father, right?"

She nodded. "I'm sorry about everything that happened, Angelo," she said. "I needed to get you here, and now you need to do the right thing with these people."

"Who is it, Barbara?" Angelo asked.

Barbara looked at Rucker. The detective shrugged.

"I don't think you know him, Angelo," Barbara said. "It's someone your father did business with. A guy from Florida."

"DeSantis? Is that who—"

"Listen," Barbara said, "this scumbag is going to be here in a little while. Josh is going to be playing you, so he needs information." She looked right at Rucker. "You help with this, and I'm certain these fine New York City Police detectives will take that into consideration, right?" Rucker nodded.

"You can help yourself a lot tonight, Mr. Telentino," Rucker said. "As long as you don't bullshit us on any of this. Tell the truth and we'll put a word in with the DA."

"Not that anything I say matters," Josh said, "but you have two choices, Angelo. Make a deal with the police or risk a trial for killing a popular young priest."

Junior stayed quiet for a moment, then his sad puppy dog eyes looked at Barbara. "I got nothing left to lose," Junior said. "Let's get to it."

Josh got as much information as Junior had regarding his father's dealings with Billy DeSantis. The best news was that he and Billy, to Junior's knowledge at least, had never met. It shouldn't be hard for Josh to assume Junior's identity. Junior told him about his two phone conversations with DeSantis.

"So, what you're telling me is I need to be a real tough guy with him, is that right?"

"I was really pissed off when I talked to him," Junior said. "My father's dead, I find a statement saying he has $13 million with this guy, and he's trying to tell me there's no money. I threatened to bring down all kinds of shit on him."

Josh rolled over in his mind the way things had played out.

"Let me see if I've got things right in my mind," he said. "Your father called Billy and told him to bring $250,000. He did this so he could ransom the jewels, not knowing it was you who had stolen them, and, in the process, had killed Father Michael."

"For what it's worth, I'm sorry about your brother, man. No one was supposed to get hurt. That's on me," Junior said.

Josh said nothing about it, but those last three words might have cut Bobby Quattrone out of the picture, except for the aiding and abetting charge. Josh nodded his head in acknowledgment and continued. "Billy used that opportunity to kill Angelo in order to steal his account, which amounted to nearly $13 million in what was now laundered money," Josh said. "I think your cousin Carmine was a wrong place, wrong time casualty."

Junior nodded. "Yeah, we were also friends. I don't know if I have any friends left." Josh stood as Detective Lieutenant Otis came back. He took Angelo into their room for what could be a very interesting debrief. Josh wished he could sit in on that interrogation. Right now, though, he had a different fish to fry.

Between what Barbara had told him about her experience and Junior's knowledge of his father's account with DeSantis Management, Josh thought he could play the role of Angelo's angry son for a few minutes without too much problem. The police, of course, were concerned that DeSantis, likely a double murderer, wouldn't think twice about trying to take out someone else if they were trying to get in his way. Otis had told Josh that this "little game" of his could become a problem real quick.

"I know you know how to do some fancy hand-to-hand stuff," Otis said, "but expect us to come through the door in a hurry if things get nasty. You have one job: get him to admit what he did. Just make sure you don't get stuck with any needles."

Barbara changed clothes and was ready to get Billy into the room—her one job.

"Damn," Josh said. "How do you expect me to unsee that?" She wore a tight-fitting red dress that ended about eight inches above her knees and was scooped low enough in the front to distract anyone, even the bishop if he were there.

"What can I say? This is me since my junior year at Lafayette High School. You like?" she asked, doing a full turn.

"I like," he said, putting his arms around her. "I like a lot." Rucker walked in.

"You know, I'd tell you two to get a room, but you already got a room. Our eyes in the lobby just sent a text. DeSantis is on his way up. It's show time!"

"Show time," Josh said. Barbara took her position.

# CHAPTER 13

They heard the knock. Barbara took a deep breath and opened the door with the chain still in place.

"Well, lookee, lookee," DeSantis said.

Barbara slid off the chain and opened the door. "You got what we talked about?" she asked. He lifted the bag.

"Gotta admit, Betsy," he said, "you are one fine-looking piece of ass." Billy walked inside. Barbara slipped through the open door and out into the hall.

Billy didn't turn around right away when the door slammed shut. He thought she was behind him. When he did look, Josh was standing there with a wide smile on his face.

"Bet you thought you were gonna have your way with her, right?" Josh said.

"Who the fuck are you?" Billy asked.

Josh eased around him and sat in front of the window. The view was spectacular: a lush, early evening snapshot of Manhattan's Upper East Side. People paid a lot of money in New York for a view like that.

"I'm Angelo Telentino, you prick," Josh said. "And I really hope you have $13 million in your little bag there."

Billy shook his head. "Angelo, listen," he said. "I don't know how many times, and how many different ways I have to tell you this. Your father closed out his account eight months ago. I brought him the money, over $12 million in cash. I can't explain to you why you don't have his final statement showing his account closed."

"Now you listen, jerk-off," Josh said. "Here's what I know—not think—know. You were here, in the city, last week. You had dinner downstairs at this hotel, and you thought you had a good time with—What did you call her? Betsy?—You came here to see my uncle and my father. You delivered a suitcase full of money to my uncle John. You had dinner at La Luna with my father. You had pastries at Ferarra's with my father. Then, sometime after you left with my father and my cousin Carmine, you killed both of them."

"You got quite an imagination, kid," Billy said.

Josh laughed. His plan was to get Billy so angry, so flustered, that he'd make a mistake. The detectives had confirmed that both Angelo Sr. and his nephew had been injected with a paralytic neurotoxin they'd not seen before and had most likely died in under a minute. Otis and Rucker reluctantly agreed to let Josh play his role until either they got the confession that would put Billy DeSantis away for good, or they saw that Josh was in jeopardy. Josh assured them that he could handle almost anything Billy had in mind unless he used a gun from a distance or was able to get close enough to inject Josh with the same hot shot he'd used on Angelo and Carmine. Josh didn't want to use the safe word that would bring the cavalry through both doors. Instead, he just wanted Billy to implicate himself.

"You seem, on the surface at least, to be a smart guy, Billy," Josh said, his eyes on Billy's hands. As long as Billy didn't make any strange moves, he could keep this going for a while.

"Smarter than you, Angelo, that's for sure," Billy said. His hands were hanging at his sides.

"Where do you have it, Billy?" Josh asked.

"Where do I have what?"

Josh got up and put another two feet between himself and Billy DeSantis. Josh's back was to the window.

"The syringe. You know, the one with the stuff you shot into my father." Josh said. "That was your plan for tonight, right? Kill Betsy? Get out of town before anyone knew you were here? Like you did last week, when you killed my father and my cousin."

"Kill her? Are you fucking crazy?" Billy put his right hand into his pocket. "Didn't you see her? Why would I want to kill her? Fuck her again, maybe."

Josh smiled. "Again? You mean like you thought you did last week? When you weren't here? What's in the bag, Billy?"

"This?" he lifted the gym bag he held in his left hand.

"I'm guessing it's, let's see, maybe $100,000? I'm just guessing, Billy. You know, I was with her when she called you yesterday. Heard every word."

Billy smiled. "This is a bunch of bullshit," he said. "I do business with a whole lot of people you don't want to have anything at all to do with. One phone call and nobody will find even a small piece of you. You think your asshole father was the first client of mine who turned up dead under mysterious circumstances? You got no fucking idea who you're dealing with."

"Okay," Rucker said, in the room next door. "We've got him."

Josh saw Billy's right hand moving inside his pocket. He took a step forward and kicked Billy hard in the left shin. Billy dropped the bag. Josh moved another step closer. Before Billy could remove his hand from his pocket, Josh nailed him in the solar plexus and then jabbed Billy in the soft tissue of his throat, just behind Billy's chin. The result was immediate.

Billy DeSantis dropped to his knees just as Quinn Otis, Marge Rucker, and Barbara came through the connecting door to the suite on the left. The tactical team from the Emergency Services Unit came in through the door on the right. Rucker cuffed Billy while Barbara leaped across the bed to get to Josh.

"I'm fine, Barbara," he said as she threw her arms around his neck.

"I know, I know," she said. "I know."

"It's over. I think," Josh said.

One of the tactical team guys frisked the prisoner. "Be careful, officer," Josh said. "Check his right thigh very carefully."

"What the fuck, Angelo?" Billy said. "You're working with cops?"

Rucker laughed. The officer felt around on Billy's thigh. He cut the pant leg away and carefully removed the syringe taped to the front of Billy's leg.

"Hey," Billy said. "Those are $300 slacks."

"He still thinks you're Angelo Telentino," Rucker said to Josh. "You got a career in acting, man."

"Maybe we should let the real Angelo have a few minutes with him," Josh said.

"You're a cop," Billy said to Josh.

"Worse than that," Rucker said, still laughing. "He's a reporter. You got done by a fucking reporter, douchebag."

Otis stood in front of Billy. "William DeSantis, you're under arrest for the murders of Angelo Telentino and Carmine Calabrese and probably a dozen or so other felonies. You have the right to remain silent." Otis finished Mirandizing Billy while they walked out of the suite. Another team of officers escorted Junior out of the room next door.

"Hey, DeSantis," Angelo yelled.

"Who the fuck are you?" Billy asked.

"Your worst fucking nightmare," Angelo said. "Especially if you and me happen to be in the same cell at the Tombs and you don't have your fancy drugs with you."

Otis took the moment. He turned Billy around. "I guess I should formally introduce the two of you fine gentlemen," he said. "Billy DeSantis, meet Angelo Telentino Jr."

The chief of security for the Sherry-Netherland escorted the cops and the criminals to a large service elevator. It took everyone to the basement. From there, they left the hotel through a door that led to a delivery bay, so as not to disturb or upset the residents and guests at the posh Fifth Avenue hotel.

The moment they got into the elevator, Billy DeSantis said the word "lawyer" over and over again.

"How many lawyers you want?" Rucker asked. "We got you here at the Sherry, sound and pictures! Witnesses put you at La Luna, at Ferrara's, at the bishop's office, and probably at Penn Station as soon as we review security tapes there. We're going to compare your prints to several we found in Telentino's Escalade. We both know how that's going to turn out. You might need a whole shitload of lawyers, you know? And none of them are gonna keep you from life without parole."

"You know," Otis said, piling on, "I think the feds are going to be interested in this piece of shit too. What was that he said? You know, about all the people he does business with? I'll bet there's a whole boatload of laundered money and a whole boatload of douchebags involved."

"Yeah," Rucker said. "And all those people? They're not gonna be real happy when all that money gets confiscated. How much shit is gonna hit how many fans?"

Billy was silent.

"Hey, DeSantis," Rucker said, "you might get to stay alive in solitary if you learn the words to all those songs you're going to have to sing when the feds come calling."

"Lawyer" was the only reply out of Billy DeSantis's mouth.

Josh and Barbara went down to the lobby bar and waited until the cops, the tech people, the two who were arrested, and the assistant DA who'd approved the whole operation left the Sherry. None of the guests were any the wiser.

They sat in silence nursing Bellinis and a light dinner and considered what might be next once all the dust settled.

"I'm exhausted," Barbara said, but she said it with a smile.

Josh looked at her. "You know, in some weird way, this whole thing was kind of fun. I mean—"

"Fun? *Fun?* You've got strange ideas about fun, Mr. Abrahams. What's weird is that everything that's gone down, from the day after Easter when . . ." She put her hand on his. "I wish you could have met Father Mike."

"Yeah," Josh said, "me too. But truly, I'm happy having met the people I've met here in . . . *the city.* Especially . . ." He took her hand and kissed it.

She smiled. "Okay," she said. "Any more of that and we're going back upstairs."

Josh spent the morning transcribing notes and recollections. He called Jasper and briefed his editor about the events surrounding his time in New York. For the moment, he left out anything involving Barbara Quattrone. Every time he thought of her, he had to stop.

She was who she was. She'd done what she'd done. He decided he was fine with all that. In fact, they connected on so many levels that he was seriously considering a future that included her. It appeared her brother was going to be at Patrick Fenton for several years. And, unless they were misreading things, her business in New York had ended abruptly with the unexpected demise of Mr. T. She said several times that she had no interest in working for Joey Sitriani or any other "mobbed up mutt," as she referred to most of the men in her current circle. She actually said a smaller town might be nice.

Until he came to New York, Josh had never thought of St. Louis as anything resembling a small town.

Jasper told Josh the nearly four-thousand-word story he'd sent in would run in the *Post*'s Sunday "A" section, beginning on page one, above the fold, with a jump to an additional two pages just before editorials and op-eds. For art, they would use photos of both Telentino brothers, Junior, Josh, and Father Mike. For her safety, and in consideration of Bobby's deal, he wrote of Barbara's role in the events of the past several days as that of an "anonymous NYPD confidential informant inside the Telentino organization."

Jasper also freed Josh to pitch the book version to the *Post*'s corporate publishing partner on Madison Avenue.

Bishop Telentino had returned the family jewels to the safe deposit box the church kept at the Valley National Bank on Avenue M. He had learned everything he needed to know from Joseph Lambert at Jacobus Jewels.

The jewels, as it turned out, had about as much intrinsic value as John had originally thought; they were mostly roughly cut colored and stained glass, with a hand-tooled linkage that connected them to one another in a fashion consistent with work done in northern Italy in the fourteenth and fifteenth centuries. The smaller stones—pearls, sapphires, rubies, and emeralds—made the arrangement worth something, but that was only one way of looking at them.

"The other way of assessing value," Joseph Lambert had told John, "is to understand that the jewels are, as is revealed through tiny markings on several of the larger red stones, directly connected to members of both the Borgia and Cattanei families, who held positions of major historical significance and infamy in Italy."

Joseph Lambert had offered to shop the jewels to the Vatican Museum, to a handful of other museums both in and outside Italy, and to some wealthy private European collectors. Several, he believed, would pay a considerable amount for them.

"Certainly seven, maybe even low eight figures," he said.

"I have a great deal to think about," John told him. "I'll send you my personal check for the appraisal. Thank you, Mr. Lambert. I promise to be in touch."

The morning after the events at the Sherry, John met with Barbara and Bobby Quattrone.

"Lieutenant Otis said, based on my nephew's official statement, that you'll be able to negotiate a plea with the DA," John said to Bobby. "I've secured a place for you at the same seminary near St. Louis where both I and Father Michael trained. While you're there, you'll need to complete a few academic prerequisites at St. Louis University; it's a Jesuit school, a good one. And then, Bobby, if you can handle the rigor, you can study for the priesthood. I must tell you, this is a very good outcome from a very bad decision you made."

Barbara could have kissed the bishop, but she knew that would be wrong on so many levels. She said, "Listen, Bobby—"

"How soon can I start?" Bobby asked. He turned to his sister. "I've thought about this for a long time, Barbara. You know I love the Church. This is perfect for me. Maybe I shouldn't say this, but it doesn't even feel like punishment."

Barbara hugged him and thanked the bishop, but without the kiss.

"I'm going to be seeing our young Mr. Abrahams later today, Barbara," John said. "Have the two of you talked about . . . anything?"

She liked him referring to them as "the two of you."

"We've talked a lot, Bishop," she said. "I have a few things I need to do before I can move on, and Josh needs to sort out whether he's going to stay with the newspaper or write a book or maybe do both."

"Do you see a future together?" the bishop asked.

She laughed. "You know, we've really only known each another for like five minutes. Speaking for myself, I'd like nothing better, Your Excellency."

"You need to schedule some time with Father James," he said, smiling. "You have some confessing to do, Barbara!"

# CHAPTER 14

The bishop and the reporter met later that afternoon at St. Brendan's. To Josh, it was time to say thank you and to establish the connective tissue necessary for follow up meetings and phone calls. These interactions might be required to help him finish the book, which he'd begun to outline and was tentatively titled *Family Jewels*.

The bishop saw the meeting as something entirely different.

Josh parked his rental car alongside the schoolyard at St. Brendan's. A group of young African American men were playing three-on-three basketball. When he got out of his car, the players stopped their game and stared at him. Deshaun walked over to the fence.

"Damn," he said. "You know, you look just like . . ." He stopped.

"I know," Josh said. "He was my twin brother." They all smiled.

"We had a running game here," Deshaun said. "He was a good guy, your brother . . . the Father."

Josh opened the gate and walked onto the court. "I know he was a good guy. The real question is: Was he a good player?" He gestured for the ball. As soon as it was passed to him, he moved a step to his left, took a single quick dribble, pulled up, and nailed a twenty-foot jump shot. The players went nuts laughing, slapping hands, and trash talking about how Father Mike kept making Deshaun pay for defensive mistakes.

"Yeah," the kid said. "He could play."

"I'm guessing a two-guard, right?" Josh asked.

"Yeah, definitely not a point guard," the big guy, Marquis, said. "Dude didn't know how to pass the ball once he got his hands on it."

Josh told them he had played in a fraternity league while getting his degree in journalism at the University of Missouri.

The group quieted down when they saw the bishop walk up to the fence. Josh said his goodbyes to the last people his brother had spent time with before the attack. He and the bishop walked east on Avenue O, past the twin staircases leading up to the entrance of St. Brendan's.

"Father James says they're good kids," John said. "He told me they liked your brother a lot."

"Interesting we both played basketball," Josh said. "I guess I'll always wonder what else we had in common."

"Let's take a walk around the block," John said. "I need to tell you a story." They crossed Avenue O and headed up E. 13th Street toward Avenue N.

"I remember the date, of course," John said. "It was a Tuesday, September 7, 1982. My mother was dying. My brother was at our Uncle Vito's candy store in Bensonhurst." He pointed to his left. "That's on the other side of McDonald Avenue.

"There was a young woman living with us. Her name is Violetta Mazzarese. She's from the old country, Siena. She was my mother's friend's niece. She came over here to help Angelo and me care for our mother. At the time, I had finished at St. John's and was waiting to go to Patrick Fenton. Angelo was already working in the—I guess I should call it the family business.

"My mother told me to call my brother at Uncle Vito's. 'Tell him to come home now, Johnny,' she said to me. 'There's not much time.' I'm not sure what I was thinking. I threw open the window to her bedroom and screamed at the top of my lungs for him. 'Angelo, Angelo.' He was maybe three blocks away; there was no way he could have heard me. I called my Uncle Vito's store and told him, 'Tell Angelo to get home, now.' Then I hung up on him.

"You have to understand, Joshua, normally I was

very polite to my Uncle Vito. My brother learned most of his criminal tendencies and tactics, I suppose, from Vito Calabrese. Well, this time I just told him to do it and hung up the phone.

"Violetta came in and started crying. She was nineteen, deaf, absolutely beautiful, and totally committed to doing whatever my mother needed. You know, bathroom, shower, food, medicine, getting dressed, getting undressed, everything. My mother told her to leave us alone for a few minutes.

"I already told you about the jewels," he said. "But I also told you there was something else . . . something else that happened that day."

Josh was perceptive, with good reporter's instincts, but he had no clue where John was going with any of this. "Why are you telling me this, sir?" he asked.

"Patience, Joshua," John said. "I put the jewels into a locked drawer in my room where they would be safe until I left for St. Louis. I had a plane ticket for the following Monday, one-way.

"My brother came home just in time for my mother to give us envelopes containing paperwork for those bank accounts I told you about that had been set up with a financial services firm in Florida, DeSantis Management."

"Not Billy DeSantis," Josh said.

"No, no, he'd have been just a kid at the time," John said. "His father, Pietro, Pete DeSantis, was part of our extended family, and, until his death, was one of the most honorable men I knew. He had mostly bad-guy clients, but he, himself, was a very good man. My brother tried to talk me out of mine, of course, but in the end, both of us did very well, even after Pete died and Billy took over. Up until last week, anyway.

"My mother died later that afternoon," John said. "We both knew it was coming. She'd been sick for well over a year and stopped the treatments when her doctor told her they were likely causing more harm than good. It was cancer, first in her colon, then the pancreas and the liver. Nasty business.

"Violetta was inconsolable that night and most of the next day," he went on. "I handled all of the arrangements although everything had been decided well in advance. My brother was happy to let me do this. He had other things on his mind."

The two men walked in silence for a few minutes. Josh had a million questions but had learned early on in his career that the best thing he could do when someone was talking was to keep his own mouth shut.

"I came home after making the arrangements at church and at the funeral home," he said. "I found Violetta on the floor of the hallway in front of the living room, barely conscious. There was blood, a lot of blood."

"I'm afraid to ask," Josh said.

"She'd been raped," he said. "It was bad. I knew immediately who it was. My brother had been trying for a long time to—"

"Bishop, you don't need to tell me this," Josh said.

"Actually, I do," he said. "I do."

They walked up E. 13th Street to Avenue N, then back down E. 12th Street. John finally stopped across the street from where Father Mike had been attacked. There was a stoop, three steps that led to a heavy wooden door that was painted red. There were stone flowerpots on either side of the steps. Impatiens and pansies made an inviting entrance to the old prewar three-story house. A silver BMW 3 Series was parked in the driveway. John sat on the second step and gestured for Josh to join him.

"I knocked at this door when I first got to the scene," Josh said, "but there was no answer."

John nodded. "My mother was already at the funeral home," he said. "Mass was scheduled. Violetta didn't want police involved. I was afraid that, if I saw my brother, I'd do something that would mess up any chance I had to go to seminary. I collected Violetta and her belongings and, with Jimmy Wakely's permission, moved her into the sisters' quarters in the rectory at St. Brendan's."

Josh struggled to process everything the bishop was sharing with him. *Why is he telling me all of this?* he thought.

"After Mass, we took my mother to Green-Wood Cemetery and buried her in a plot with my father. They were joined later on by Uncle Vito, followed by one of his brothers, then by Vito's wife, my mother's sister. My father's sister, who died during childbirth before my brother and I were born, is buried there too. Now Angelo is buried there. Honestly, I'm not sure if I'll be buried there or not. That whole family, I just . . . I just don't know."

"I hope you don't have to concern yourself about that for a long time, sir," Josh said. He didn't know what else to say.

"The next day, Violetta and I took a flight to St. Louis. Jimmy helped with the arrangements for her to heal with the sisters at Patrick Fenton. Jimmy's been a good friend for as long as I can remember."

The bishop stood up. Josh headed down the steps thinking they were continuing their walk.

"About a month after we arrived at the seminary," John said, "we learned that Violetta was pregnant. About two months after that, we learned she was carrying twins."

Josh spun around and stared at John. "You're telling me—"

"I'm telling you that, for better or for worse, Joshua, you're my nephew. Angelo Jr. is your half brother. At least some of the money still sitting in my brother's account with DeSantis could be yours when the lawyers, the police, the FBI, and the IRS are done fighting over it. All of mine, at the time of my passing, will be left to you, and"—he smiled broadly— "whoever may happen to be in your life when that day comes."

Josh sat back down. He was dizzy. The bishop smiled.

"Those jewels, the ones that started this whole thing—someday I'll be passing them along to you as well," John said. "It turns out they are, in fact, quite valuable, but they need to stay in our family, Joshua. That's you. I know you'll do the right thing with them."

John stood on a step above Josh. He put his hands on Josh's shoulders. "I know it's a lot, Josh," he said. "I spoke to your parents the day before yesterday. They send their love."

Joshua's head was spinning. "My parents?" he asked.

"I needed their permission for this."

He turned and put a key into the lock on the front door.

"Joshua," the bishop said, "there's someone upstairs here who very much wishes to meet you."


-End-

# ACKNOWLEDGMENTS

The author would like to thank so, so many people who have knowingly or otherwise supported this effort, including the Katz, Medlar, Diehn, and Van Oss families; friends and colleagues in both western North Carolina and central Florida; professors and fellow students at Valencia College, Rollins College, and Western Carolina University; and even a few from long ago in Brooklyn, New York, and the United States Air Force. Some may recognize pieces and aspects of themselves on these and pages, while others may wonder why they've been forgotten. They haven't.

Thanks to Robert Kenney of Thoughtful Editing, Victoria Griffin, and Anna Krusinski from Blue Pen. Thanks to Ron Rash, Pam Duncan, Bob Morris, and Steven Cooper for their wisdom, advice, counsel, and encouragement. Special thanks always to Lynn for putting up with all the hours of closed doors and quiet keystrokes emanating from the back room.

# ABOUT THE AUTHOR

Bruce F. Katz – Bud to his friends – is author of the business biography, *When Your Name Is On the Door*, along with five novels, a novella, and more than a dozen short stories. He was graduated Magna Cum Laude from Western Carolina University with a BA in English. He's a former strategic communication, mass media, advertising and public relations executive living with his wife, Lynn, a retired defense and aerospace industry executive, in Highlands, North Carolina.